HIDDEN THIRST

Doug & Amy Palmer

HIDDEN THIRST

ISBN: 978-0-9859920-0-2

Cover art by Shankombo Chikonka

Printed in the United States of America

Disclaimer:
This story is for the sole purpose of entertainment, and is not based on
any other known literary work or performance. All characters are
fictional and do not represent real persons living or deceased.
References to organizations such as NASA do not represent their views
or any actual research findings.

We dedicate this book to Kay Palmer,
with more love than all the ocean's waves.

HIDDEN THIRST
An original work of fiction

This science fiction thriller mixes modern mysteries of science, faith, and ancient mythology with a generous dose of the probing question, "What if?"

The twists and turns of the story evolved as a long-term father-daughter writing project, created for the reading entertainment of those who like adventure, suspense, and humor.

INTRODUCTION

NASA Scientist Jo Kendesh and her team discover something Earth shattering, and for the sake of humanity, they have to figure out how to deal with it. As the dilemma grows, a tangled web of international drama unfolds.

What would happen if this discovery became public? Who should know about it, and what emergency steps should be taken? What if this knowledge fell into the wrong hands?

With the very existence of life as we know it in peril, the adventure begins...

CONTENTS

Chapter 1

Mission Control

After a tiring day at the NASA Space Center in Houston, Texas, research scientist Jo Kendesh attended an evening, Ash Wednesday, church service. The priest declared, "Remember man that you are dust and to dust you shall return," as he applied symbolic ashes to her forehead. Jo had no idea that this humble reminder of her mortality would be an ironic beginning for what was about to unfold.

When the service was over Jo rushed home, kicked off her shoes, and plopped on the couch to relax and read the local paper. It had been a long day, and she knew it would be an even longer night.

The front page featured an article titled, "Comet Study Under Way." It outlined NASA's latest space exploration mission intended to gain a better understanding of the origins of the universe and perhaps life itself.

Three years ago, Jo's research associates and friends, Rick Johnson and Jason Taylor, discovered a comet, which was named after them.

The article went on to explain that the large, fast approaching Johnson-Taylor Comet would be passing through our solar system at a time when the Earth's position would be perfect for the study of the comet's structure.

It also explained that ten months ago a small craft called "Starsweep" was launched to cross paths with the comet. The probe would send information back to Earth about the comet's size, shape, and magnetic field properties.

This information was important, but for Jo and her coworkers the most exciting part of the mission will be the safe return of sample material from the comet's tail.

This would be the first time since the Apollo moon missions that something from outer space would be brought directly back to Earth for study.

For a long time the thought of being the first to investigate material no one has ever seen before had been keeping the whole mission team from getting a good night's sleep. Much like the scientists chosen to study moon rock samples, they knew their work would become an important part of history because this opportunity was rare.

As Jo read the news article and began to doze off, the phone rang.

With a startled flinch, she grabbed the phone and answered, "Hello?"

"Hi Jo, it's Rick. Do you plan to come back tonight and follow the intercept?"

She asked, "Are you kidding? We've waited forever for this! Of course I'm coming back, but I thought I'd check my mail and hit a drive through on the way. Can I bring you and Jason anything?"

Rick replied, "Sure, but make it something light. We don't need any more stomach troubles than we already have."

"I hear ya! The closer Starsweep moves toward the comet, the more tense everyone gets. The probe passes through the main part of the comet's tail about 11:30 P.M., so I'll be in around 11:00. We're all counting on a smooth sample collection and a good booster rocket burn. I wouldn't miss that for the world!"

"Thanks Jo, we'll see you then."

As Jo hung up the phone and sorted the day's mail, she could not help thinking about how critical the return rocket burn would be. The probe was to pass through the comet's tail while being very near the comet itself. The small craft's path would be turned back toward Earth by the comet's gravity. After the craft curves around the comet, a booster rocket will help speed the probe back home.

It took ten months for the comet and the probe to cross paths, but with the booster rocket and Earth's orbit moving in the direction of the approaching comet, the return trip will only take two weeks.

Fortunately, the comet will be passing the earth at a very great distance so there is no danger of a collision. It will actually come closer to Mars than to Earth. In fact, Jo recalled Jason explaining that the supercomputer models of the comet path show a very near miss with Mars millions of years ago. He said in its early history evidence leaned toward Mars being covered with water much like the earth is today. This comet would have passed close enough to send huge tidal waves ripping across the ancient Martian seas. Imagine the wake from a speedboat the size of Texas. The waves would have been miles high and would have traveled half way around the planet. Where water didn't cover the surface, the huge comet flying past would have caused hurricane force windstorms to blast across the landscape.

As the solar system continued to form and planet orbits slowed, the comet's path ended up being what exists today. This made it a perfect object to gather samples from and study.

On Jo's way back to mission control, she stopped at a drive through and picked up some roast beef sandwiches and black coffee. She thought to herself that if this stuff were too much for their stomachs she would share the antacids she always carries in her pocket.

After sliding her security card through the gate slot and entering her identification code on the keypad, the gates opened and she drove to her usual parking space. It was not unusual for the night security guard to see Jo and other members of the project team come and go at all hours. With a little wave while saying "Hey Sam," she passed by the guard desk and entered the control room.

"Here's dinner guys. How's Starsweep doing?"

While still intently looking at his monitor, Rick announced, "Looks like we've lucked out so far. Everything's on schedule, and I could eat a horse. What did you bring us?"

"Well, they were out of horse, so cow and coffee will have to do." She set the bags and cups by their workstations and focused on the huge tracking board that displayed the progress of the comet and the Starsweep probe.

Rick looked up and questioned, "What's on your forehead?"

While she studied the craft's progress on the tracking board she replied, "It's Ash Wednesday. You know, the ashes signify that we came from dust and we'll end up as dust."

With a chuckle Jason joked, "Oh yeah? Maybe we should test the Starsweep's dust samples for a DNA match with you."

Jo looked at Jason with one eyebrow raised, smiled and said, "If that comet dust has DNA, I call dibs on the Nobel Prize."

In a few minutes they would know if their years of planning and hard work would pay off with the successful collection of comet material. If all goes as planned, shield doors will open on the probe as it passes through the pick up zone of the comet's tail. The open doors will expose a chamber where debris from the tail stream will be captured, much like a vacuum cleaner filter collects dirt.

After that, their attention can be turned to the booster rocket ignition so the probe can be successfully brought back home. If the booster doesn't work as it should the probe will spin off into deep space and be lost forever. Years and years of hard work and millions of dollars will have gone to waste. In the eyes of the NASA team, this would not be a pretty picture.

While Rick chewed on his pencil like an ear of corn, a distant sounding voice came over the speakerphone at Jo's workstation. "Mission control, our readings indicate Starsweep has successfully opened the collection bay doors and is now picking up material from the comet's tail."

Jo shouted, "Yes!" and swung her fist through the air as if to strike a knockout punch.

Rick chuckled nervously while a group of workers in the control room clapped their hands in approval.

The voice over the speaker then continued, "Mission control, booster rocket to fire in five minutes from my mark." A short pause was followed by "T minus three-hundred seconds and counting."

As Rick anxiously looked around the room, then back at Jo he said, "Well, this is it. If everyone has done their homework we'll be pulling Starsweep out of the ocean in two weeks."

Looking up at the huge progress screen Jo whispered under her breath, "Come on baby, bring that cargo home!"

All eyes in the control room were locked on the progress board. A flashing white dot on the huge screen represented the Starsweep, which was slowly curving around the comet and heading back in the direction of Earth. The only sound in the room was a faint beep every ten seconds as the countdown continued.

Suddenly, the voice on the speaker broke the silence with, "T minus ten seconds and counting to booster fire." Everyone in the room held their breath as the voice then called out.

"Five, four, three, two, one…ignition."

The tracking animation on the progress screen turned from white to red at the spot where Starsweep was located. This showed the booster engine was firing to accelerate toward earth.

The voice over the speaker announced, "Mission control, the rocket has fired as planned. The Starsweep probe is headed home. Good work team."

Rick looked at Jo and yelled, "All right!" Giving her a big hug he lifted her and spun around. Cheers erupted around the control room as people exchanged high fives and celebrated.

During the excitement, the special phone connected to the U.S. Naval Observatory rang several times before Jo heard it and picked it up. Since the Vice President of the United State's official residence was located at the observatory, she knew this would be an important call.

Covering the receiver she shouted, "Hey everyone, quiet down!"

Jason also yelled over the noise, "Quiet, it's the observatory!"

Rick watched intently while Jo waved her arm at those still making noise. She covered her open ear, listened for a short time on the line then said, "Thank you sir… yes sir, we're very pleased with the mission progress too. In two weeks we splashdown in the Pacific Ocean. Yes sir. We'll keep you posted."

Jo hung up and Rick asked, "Well, what did he say?"

She raised her voice so the whole room could hear, "The Vice President of the United States said congratulations, and he asked when the probe will be back to Earth. Then he said to keep up the good work and get some rest!"

Rick laughed, "Rest?" Pointing at the coffee cups on the desk he said, "After drinking that mud we won't be able to sleep for a week! Let's call our buddies in the recovery group and finalize the details for picking Starsweep up."

"At this hour? Actually Rick, I'm exhausted. Coffee or not, I feel like I could sleep for a month, so I'm headed home. I'll call you tomorrow and we'll get the splashdown details from Mike."

"You're right. Mike wouldn't be happy if we woke him to say, 'Welcome to the no-sleep-for-you club.'"

Mike Watson, who is head of the probe recovery team, will be filling Jo's group in on the probe recovery procedures.

As Jo threw her trash from dinner away she said, "Thanks guys," waved to the overnight tracking crew, and went out the door.

When she got back to her apartment the answering machine was beeping with a message.

She hit the play button and heard, "Hello Miss Kendesh, my name is Susan McCalum, and I'm with the International Broadcasting Company. I would like to set up an interview with you regarding the Starsweep space project. Please call my office at your earliest convenience, and we'll set up an appointment. The number is 678-4312, extension 45. Thank you."

As Jo wrote the caller's name and number on a note pad she asked herself, "Why not?" She knew the project needed as much exposure as possible if the agency hoped to gain support for more funding.

Right now the only thing on her mind was a good night's sleep. She set her alarm for 9:00 A.M., shut off the phone ringer, and turned out the light.

It seemed she had just closed her eyes when the alarm went off with an annoying BUZZZ.

Jo rolled over and turned off the alarm. Groaning, she sat up in bed and noticed the answering machine light was flashing, which indicated a message came in while the phone ringer was off.

Pushing the play button she heard Rick say in a sleepy sounding voice, "Hey Jo, it's Rick. Mike just called to say he wants to meet us at 1:00 this afternoon for a briefing on the Starsweep splashdown. I reminded him it would be two weeks before it gets back, but he said he wants to make sure all the details are covered. Give me a call, and I'll fill you in."

Jo hit the auto-dial button for Rick's number and after three rings she heard, "Leave a message after the beep. If I'm here and I can get to the phone I'll pick up, if I don't answer, leave your number and I'll get back to you."

BEEP.

"Hey Rick its Jo. I know you're home, pick up your beeping phone."

A crashing, fumbling sound came across the line followed by, "Wait, hey, I'm here." Clunk, bang, "Hang on!"

With a laugh in her voice Jo said, "Did I wake you?"

Rick replied, "Oh man, what time is it?"

"It's about 9:15. How much sleep have you had?"

"Well, I got home about 4:00 A.M., Mike called and woke me up around 6:00, I left you a message and now it's 9:15? You do the math."

"Sorry to wake you, but you said Mike wants to get a jump on the recovery briefing at one o'clock?"

"Yeah, I tried to talk him into meeting later but he's anxious for us to be ready. He called Jason about the meeting too. I think he just wants us to cross all our i's and dot all the t's."

Shaking her head, smiling and crossing her eyes at what Rick just said in his sleepless daze, she shared, "I had a message from the media when I got home. They want to set up an interview for an update on Starsweep's progress."

"That's great Jo! After we meet with Mike you'll have more details on the landing. Some good media promotion would fit right in. We need all the press we can get if we want our work to continue."

Jo replied, "That's what I was thinking too. Now get some sleep. I'll stop by for you around noon so we can meet Mike at one o'clock. I'll try to set up the interview for sometime afterward."

"Thanks Jo. I'll see you about noon. Just keep ringing the doorbell until I answer."

Jo hung up and got ready for another hectic day. After wolfing down a bowl of cold cereal, she dialed the number to arrange her media interview.

After two rings she heard, "Good morning, and welcome to the International Broadcasting Company phone system. IBC wishes to provide the highest level of service to our customers, so please pick the department you wish to contact from the following menu."

Jo mumbled to herself, "Yada, yada, yada, let's get on with it."

"If you wish to contact our sales and promotion department, enter the number one, followed by the pound sign. If you wish to contact our production group, enter the number two, followed by the pound sign. If you wish to contact...."

After listening to eight more entry possibilities, the recording said, "And if you know the extension of the person you would like to contact please enter star, then the number, followed by the pound sign."

By this time Jo was losing her patience and complained, "Why didn't they say that in the first place?" Then she added under her breath, "I'll give you the pound sign."

She entered *45# and the line began to ring.

When the line was picked up she heard, "Hello, you've reached the office of reporter Susan McCalum. Please leave a message and your number after the tone and I'll get back to you as soon as I can. Thanks and have a great day!"

BEEP.

"Hi, this is Jo Kendesh, the Starsweep space probe project leader. You left a message wanting to set up an interview? I have a meeting this afternoon at one, so I'll call again later to set something up."

Jo hung up and decided to call Jason to be sure he was ready for the one o'clock meeting as well. She dialed his number and prayed she wouldn't have to listen to another answering machine message. It began to ring and she heard, "Hello?"

"Hi Jason, it's Jo. Are you ready to meet with Mike and the recovery group at one?"

"Yeah, he called me at some ungodly hour this morning to say we needed to be there. I think he was going to call Rick too."

"He did. I just talked to Rick and I'll be picking him up at noon. I guess we'll see you at Mike's office then."

"Sounds good. Hey before I forget, thanks for all your help with this Jo. We've got a good group of people working on this project, and I think it's gone this well so far because you're part of it."

"Thanks Jason, but we've got a long way to go before we can pat ourselves on the back. I won't get a full night's sleep until Starsweep is back here in one piece and we're making discoveries about what your comet is composed of in the lab."

"You and me both, Jo. We'll see what Mike's got in store for us at one."

"Okay Jason, sounds good."

After hanging up, she checked her e-mail.

While her laptop booted up she poured a glass of orange juice and thumbed through a stack of mail on the coffee table. There she saw the usual bills, magazines, and junk mail.

The computer beeped, indicating it was up and running, then she logged on to her e-mail account.

Much like the regular mail stack, most of the messages were junk. There were several jokes passed on by friends, ads for on-line banking, and a message from her mom.

This one caught her interest since her mom was normally very shy about sending e-mail. Jo opened the message and it read, "Dear Jo, Congratulations on the news of Starsweep heading home! May your project enjoy continued success. Your dad and I are very proud of you, and we're looking forward to hearing about your discoveries. Love, Mom & Dad."

With all the hectic work leading up to this point she realized she had not been in contact with her folks in quite a while. She hit the reply icon and typed, "Dear Mom & Dad, thanks for your note. I appreciate your support! I've been so busy lately that I haven't had time to get in touch. I won't rest easy until the Starsweep is safely back on Earth and the comet samples are in my lab. I promise you'll be among the first to know what we discover. Take care, Love, Jo."

She no more than hit the send button when her phone rang.

"Hello?" she answered.

"Hello, Jo? This is Susan McCalum with IBC. How are you?"

"Fine thanks, I'm glad you called. I understand you'd like an interview on the comet probe's progress?"

"Yes, we'd like to ask a few questions about Starsweep for a news program that will air next Tuesday evening. Can we count on you?"

"Sure! By then the probe will be well on its way back home, and we'll have more to share about the splashdown, and recovery plans. When and where would you like to meet?"

"Well, how about this afternoon, say three o'clock, at the IBC studios on Central Avenue?"

Jo responded, "That sounds fine."

"Great! The interview should last about twenty minutes. Plan on the whole process taking about two hours though, since we'll be messing with lights and make-up. Just ask for me at the front desk."

"Sounds fine, what should I wear?"

"I'm sure whatever you normally wear at NASA will be fine."

At that point, Jo knew the reporter probably had no clue what she was saying. If she was expecting a lab coat with pocket protector, thick dark rimmed glasses and a clipboard she was in for a surprise. Would the jeans, sweat shirt and ball cap that she often wore be appropriate?

Searching for a more definite answer Jo asked, "Business casual?"

"That would be fine, I'll be looking for you at three o'clock. Thanks Jo."

"Thank you Susan, I'll see you this afternoon."

Jo knew she needed to put more gas in her car before she picked up Rick, so it was time to leave. Grabbing her jacket and keys, out the door she went.

On the way to the station, she flipped the radio on and there was a talk show in progress with a caller complaining about the money the government is spending on projects like the Starsweep.

The caller said, "Who cares what comets are made of? What value is there in spending millions of dollars on space ships when the money could be used to repair bridges and build schools?"

The show host responded, "Your point is well taken, but I would hope what they learn from doing this kind of science becomes part of what they teach in our schools."

To this the caller replied, "Well, I think it's a pure wasta tax dollars to mess with dis nonsense. When I went to school, readin', writin' and 'rithmetic were all we needed. If it was good 'nuf then, it should be good 'nuf now! Dat's all I got to say."

The host announced, "Thanks, and we'll be right back to take more of your calls after these messages. This is Pat Simon on, 'Your Forum.'"

Jo shook her head in disbelief at what she was hearing. She was glad to hear the host touch on a key reason for studying the composition of comets though.

She believed that the more knowledge humankind could gain and pass on about the universe around us, the better off future generations would be. As the old saying goes, knowledge is power.

After a series of commercials on the radio ended, the show host took another caller.

"Hello, and welcome to 'Your Forum.'" What's your name and what's on your mind?"

"Hi Pat, my name is Judy and I'd like to say your last caller was an idiot! I think if everyone felt the way he did, we'd all be nomads wandering the countryside, picking berries, and hunting for food with rocks and clubs."

The show host asked, "Where do you think we need to draw the line on what's paid for with public funding, Judy?"

She responded, "Well, that's a tough question but who can say where or when the next major discovery will be made that could change our world for the better?

I read somewhere that for each dollar spent on NASA projects, there's about a five-dollar return based on the development of technologies used to make the new discoveries. I'm just saying I'd rather see tax money spent on learning new things to make the world a better place, than spent on going nowhere with the status quo."

The host concluded with, "Thanks Judy, we appreciate your call. That's all the time we have for today. This is Pat Simon signing off and we'll be back taking your calls again tomorrow on, 'Your Forum.'"

Jo turned off the radio as she pulled into the gas station and hopped out of the car. Fortunately, Rick's house was nearby.

She ran her credit card through the pump, and while filling the tank she thought about how the mission was finally coming together.

The pump clicked off and Jo was brought back to the reality of needing to pick up Rick and go to Mike's splashdown meeting.

Climbing back into her car, Jo headed back out into traffic toward Rick's place. As she approached the exit she needed, her cell phone rang. Picking it up from the passenger seat she said, "Hello?"

On the line she heard, "Jo, it's Rick, where are you?"

"I'm just a few miles from your place. Traffic has me running a little late. What are you doing up? I thought you'd be sleeping like a log!"

Rick replied, "I should have been, but I couldn't get back to sleep after we talked. There's been too much going on the past few days, and now that Starsweep is on its way back home with our comet samples, I'm too wound up!"

"I know what you mean. Maybe after the splashdown meeting we need to exhaust ourselves swimming or working out at the gym. That usually helps me sleep better."

"Good idea, Jo. I'll look for you out front in a couple of minutes."

"I'm on my way, bye."

In just a few minutes Jo pulled up to the front of Rick's house as he came out the front door, pulling on his jacket while eating a donut. Getting into the passenger seat he held it toward her face and asked, "Want a bite?"

As Jo pulled away from the curb she replied, "No thanks, I'm trying to cut back. Any idea how long Mike wants to meet with us?"

"No, but once we're done we should swing by mission control and see how Starsweep is doing. You know, after all this time it's hard for me to believe this is really happening. It seems like it was ages ago that Jason and I first spotted the comet, and now in just a few days we'll be looking at some of it in the lab."

Jo nodded and said, "I hear ya. Everybody's pretty excited about the probe getting back in one piece. I spoke with the reporter from IBC and have an interview set up for three this afternoon, so if Mike isn't done with us before then I'll need you to take notes for me. We're just going to be observers at the splashdown anyway. I'm not sure why it's so important we know all the details."

As Rick licked the last donut crumbs from his fingers he said, "Mike just wants to make sure everything's done by the book. He's been doing ocean recoveries for years, and he doesn't want a good mission botched on his watch."

They pulled up to the guard gate where the recovery team was based, and Jo announced they'd arrived for a one o'clock meeting with Mike Watson. A guard came out of the station to check her ID badge and waved to have the gate opened so they could proceed. The gate opened and Jo pulled the car around to Mike's office building. They noticed Jason's car was already there, and they made their way to the conference room.

Entering the room, they saw Mike chatting with Jason as he brought up a map of the Pacific Ocean on a big screen display. About twenty people had taken their seats and the clock on the wall read it was one minute before the show would start.

Rick shouted, "Hey Mike, where's the popcorn?" A few chuckles could be heard as all eyes turned toward Rick while he and Jo made their way to seats near the front of the room.

"Hey Rick, hey Jo, I'm glad you're here. Jason was just telling me you guys had a long night making sure your craft was going to make it back safe and sound."

Jo replied, "If you can find it in the Pacific and bring it back for us we'll be in good shape."

Mike announced, "If everyone would please have a seat I'll try to make this briefing short. We're all very busy and there's not much time between now and the time we'll be pulling the Starsweep probe out of the ocean."

With a welcoming wave of his arm toward them he said, "First, I want to congratulate Jo Kendesh and her Starsweep probe team for getting things this far. It was only three years ago that Rick Johnson and Jason Taylor discovered the comet this probe was sent to study. Pulling a mission of this sort together in such a short time was a huge task. We're here today to talk about the last phase of the Starsweep's return trip home."

"The last leg of this relay isn't over until the Starsweep probe is safely back in Dr. Kendesh's lab." He continued, "If everyone keeps doing their part we plan to add a few more good pages to U.S. space history."

"Starsweep is scheduled to re-enter Earth's atmosphere over the Pacific Ocean around 9:00 A.M., February 27th. Splashdown is expected to be near 150 degrees longitude and 15 degrees north latitude. This area is about 500 miles southeast of the Hawaiian Island city of Hilo, and there's a lot of open water out there. We don't want to lose it. Our satellite, surface, and air-born radar will be used to track the craft, while Navy vessels will be used to secure the area for recovery."

"Are there any questions?"

A few hands rose among those attending, and Mike pointed to one, "Yes?"

"Since the probe is small, will it be brought back to NASA by the recovery aircraft or will it be brought back on a Navy ship?"

Mike responded, "For safety and security reasons the probe will be brought back on the same naval vessel as the NASA observation team. There's less risk of loss on the ship, and security will be greater."

Pointing to another raised hand he said, "More questions…yes?"

"Will the craft be quarantined the way the moon samples were, to prevent possible contamination?"

Mike replied, "I'll let Ms. Kendesh respond to that since she knows more about the probe than I do."

Jo stood and turned to address the group. "There are no special quarantine plans for the Starsweep probe, since the craft's exterior will be more than sterilized from high temperatures during re-entry. The comet sample material is very well protected and sealed inside the craft and this will avoid the possibility of unknown contamination."

Another hand was raised and since Jo was still standing, she took the question, "Since the space shuttles landed like glider planes, why doesn't the Starsweep probe do the same thing?"

She answered, "Cost. The Starsweep was designed as a one-time use vehicle to save money. On the other hand, the space shuttle was used again, and again, for very different purposes. Since it will be generations before comet Johnson-Taylor will pass through our solar system again, there was no reason to spend extra money to make it reusable."

Jo turned to Mike and asked, "Do you foresee any problems trying to locate and recover an object the size of a sofa, landing in thousands of square miles of ocean?"

Mike responded, "Twenty years ago I'd have said yes, but with our current radar and satellite tracking systems we shouldn't have too much trouble finding your 'sofa.' Now, if that answers everyone's questions for today, I'll run down what's supposed to happen after re-entry."

Rick interrupted, "One more quick question Mike, will the media be out there following this too?"

"Well Rick, there's no way for us to keep anyone in a boat from sailing the open ocean. The Navy will be working to keep those not involved with the recovery at a safe distance. As usual, there will be some news networks and politicians interested in the recovery but it's out in the middle of nowhere, so it's not likely going to be a big news item."

Mike continued, "The probe is equipped with a float collar and signal system that will help a Navy helicopter zero in on it. Divers will attach a cable system to the probe so it can be lifted and set down on the deck of a Navy cruiser. This is the ship the research team will be on so they can inspect the probe for damage and document its condition before we return it to the NASA lab for sample study. That's all I want to cover for today. There will be more meetings as recovery day gets closer, so I'll be in touch. Thanks for everyone's help on this, and let's keep it a trouble free mission."

With that, the room began to clear, and Jo noticed from the clock on the wall that she had plenty of time to make it to her interview at IBC.

Jo said, "Thanks Mike, before we set sail, just let us know when and where you want us to be."

Turning to Rick she said, "Can you catch a ride with Jason? After the interview I'll meet you back at mission control."

Jason replied, "No problem, we'll see you there. Good luck with the interview! We need all the media hype we can get to keep our studies going."

Rick added, "Amen to that, we'll see you in a bit."

Soon after, Jo arrived at the IBC studio offices and asked for Susan McCalum at the front desk. The receptionist rang McCalum's office and let her know the interview appointment had arrived. Then she led Jo to a small studio furnished with a coffee table and two chairs.

The receptionist said, "Susan will be with you in a few minutes. Make yourself comfortable, and one of the make-up technicians will be in shortly."

As the receptionist left, Jo took a seat and responded, "Thank you."

In a few moments, a short woman in a blue smock entered the room and said, "Hi, are you being interviewed by Susan this afternoon?"

"Yes," Jo replied.

"My name's Carol, and I need to apply some make-up so the lights don't make you look ill."

"Okay, Susan mentioned the interview would be about 20 minutes, but it would take some time to have make-up applied."

The make-up technician walked around Jo with her arms folded and her left hand on her cheek. As she circled the chair she mumbled, "Hmmm, okay, hmmm."

Jo wasn't into using much make-up so she sat up a little straighter in her chair, wondering if better posture might mean less make-up would be needed.

Carol left the room and soon returned with a wheeled cart full of jars, bottles, cans, and brushes.

Jo was amused at the thought of make-up being the price she'd have to pay to get more media exposure for projects like Starsweep.

Shortly after Carol was finished, two camera operators entered the room and began to fiddle with setting up the cameras and lights. After about five minutes Susan McCalum entered the room carrying a note pad and greeted Jo.

"Hello Jo Kendesh, it's a pleasure to meet you. Thanks for taking the time from your busy schedule to answer a few questions for us."

Jo replied, "Thanks for asking me Susan. I appreciate the chance to share what we're working on so the public can get a better feel for why it's important."

"Since our time will be limited Jo, I'd like to do a quick run-down of what I'll cover with you. First, I'll ask you to give a brief background of the project. Next, I'll ask where the mission's at today, and my final question will be what's next? Do you think we can cover all that in twenty minutes?"

"You bet. When do we start?" Jo inquired.

Susan asked the camera crew if they're ready and got a thumbs-up. She said, "If you're ready let's do it right now."

One of the camera operators called out, "3, 2, 1… and GO!"

Susan opened with, "Good evening, I'm Susan McCalum with IBC. This evening we're talking with NASA project manager, Doctor Jo Kendesh. She is the team leader for the comet research probe called Starsweep. In the next few minutes we'll learn more about what the space agency hopes to accomplish with the mission. First, can you give our audience a brief background on the Starsweep comet probe?"

Jo replied, "Certainly. Three years ago, NASA research scientists Rick Johnson and Jason Taylor discovered a large comet heading into our solar system. It turned out that the path of this comet was ideal for us to collect sample material and bring it back to Earth for study. Because of this, NASA put the Starsweep project on the fast track. We calculate the comet won't return to this part of our solar system for another 16,000 years, so we had to seize the opportunity while it existed. By the way, the tabloids will be disappointed to know there's no danger of this comet colliding with the earth."

Susan responded, "That's good to hear, but why is it important to know more about what comets are made of?"

Jo replied, "Well Susan, comets are objects that date back to the early formation of our solar system. Learning more about these ancient objects will give us a better understanding of how the solar system formed and may even help explain the origins of life. Seldom do they come close enough to study much less gather actual samples to study first hand. It just so happens at this point in our history we have a rare opportunity, and the technology, to bring comet material back to earth. Since the Apollo missions brought samples back from the moon, this will be the first time that mankind will be able to study unaltered material from deep space."

"Why would this be different from studying a meteorite that has already fallen to Earth?" Susan asked.

"Good question. Material that falls to Earth is physically and chemically changed, due to the extreme heat created during the fall through our atmosphere."

Jo went on to say, "When people see flashes of light in the night sky or streaks through the heavens, they often incorrectly call them shooting stars, when they are not really stars at all. It's simply space debris burning up in Earth's atmosphere. Most of this material doesn't even reach the ground before it vaporizes."

Continuing her explanation she said, "Comets generally exist in a distant halo that astronomers call the Oort cloud, which surrounds the outer reaches of our solar system. On rare occasions, these deep space objects travel toward the sun in an elliptical orbit. Some no more than once, and some in a repeating cycle until they eventually break up or hit another object.

A perfect example of this was the spectacular collision that took place between the Shoemaker-Levy 9 comet and Jupiter, back in 1994. That was the first time humans were able to observe such an event using equipment like the Hubble Space Telescope."

Susan responded, "This stuff is fascinating. What stage is the Starsweep mission at now?"

Jo replied, "The Starsweep probe has successfully scooped up material from the tail of comet Johnson-Taylor, and will fall to Earth in the Pacific Ocean on February 27th. Our findings will be published after we've had a chance to study the material."

"This is exciting Jo, do you have any predictions of what you'll find?" Susan asked.

"Well, we have a rough idea about what the comet is made of from the data sent back by the probe during the intercept and collection phase of the project. We have no idea what the final analysis will tell us though."

"I'm sure we'll be hearing a lot more about your team's findings in the near future Jo. Thank you and good luck with your research."

"Thanks for inviting me, Susan. I'd like to add one more quick comment. There's always been debate about where money should be spent when it comes to research like this. When an opportunity to learn more about our universe presents itself less than once in a lifetime, we need to take action. This was one of those times. Our ability to grab this comet by the tail wasn't something we could afford to miss. We're encouraging everyone to support our efforts to better understand nature."

One of the camera operators raised his hand and said, "And cut!"

Susan shook Jo's hand and said, "Thanks for your time Jo, that went very well. We'll be in touch as your discoveries unfold. I've got to run to another appointment, so I'll say goodbye."

"Thanks Susan, it's been my pleasure."

Chapter 2

Splashdown

The next several days involved tracking Starsweep as it continued to move closer to Earth. The project team spent their time studying the data sent back to Mission Control during the approach and the material pick up phase of the mission.

Preliminary data showed the Johnson-Taylor Comet to be about 400 miles in diameter, which is huge for that type of object. It also showed the comet has a stone like structure, which is very unusual. Most of them are believed to be more like large dirty snowballs, rather than small rocky moons.

This also explained why the comet did not display a bright, long tail as many do. The data would seem to show it is quite unique as far as comets go, so the thought of getting material back to Earth for closer study was becoming even more exciting.

Four days before splashdown, Jo, Rick, and Jason flew to the naval base in San Diego to board the USS Goddard. This ship was equipped with special radar and tracking systems designed to make the task of following and recovering a small spacecraft easier.

A landing platform was on the rear of the ship where the Starsweep will be secured for transport, after it is pulled from the Pacific Ocean.

An escort fleet of three additional ships would also be involved with the recovery. One will provide tracking assistance, and two are armed naval vessels to help secure the area from any interference by outside interests. Satellites and land-based observatories were also going to provide added tracking, so following and finding the probe as it descended back to Earth was not expected to be a problem.

Since the project was not classified as a military mission, nor was it a manned mission, only light support was being provided.

It certainly did not command the attention and security that the Apollo moon missions did, but the fact that the cargo was from a one-time-shot opportunity, meant it had to be treated with a certain measure of security and priority.

When it came down to it, the material the Starsweep would be bringing back to Earth will be worth more than the most precious stones in the world. Indeed, this material would be even rarer than moon rocks! Not that this comet dust would ever be offered for sale on the open market, but if it were, who could put a price on it?

As the NASA team members were getting settled into their quarters, the ships' crew continued to prepare the ship for departure.

A Navy helicopter flew in and slowly landed on the recovery platform. The crew then quickly lashed it down. Meanwhile, the tracking equipment was run through countless tests to make sure Starsweep would not end up being lost at sea.

At this point, Jo was not sure when the ship was supposed to depart, so she asked the first crewmember she saw. "Excuse me sir, what time do we set sail?"

"We leave port at fifteen-hundred hours ma'am," the crewman answered. Jo thanked him and looked at her watch to think for a minute what military time converted to on her watch. Noon is twelve-hundred hours, so fifteen-hundred would be 3:00 P.M. It is about two now, she thought, so in an hour they would leave port.

Just then Jo heard Jason's voice ask, "Ever been on a ship at sea before?"

Jo answered, "No, and that's why I brought plenty of medication for sea sickness, just in case."

"Good thinking," Jason replied. "You never know when things will get rough out there and it's hard to concentrate when you're losing your lunch over the side rail."

"Thanks for that image, Jason. Where's Rick?"

"He's making sure all the communication links to the land-based trackers are ready. We're supposed to meet him by the helicopter when the ship casts off."

Jo replied, "Let's head for the flight pad soon."

As Jo and Jason arrived at the pad, Rick was already there scanning the horizon with a huge set of binoculars mounted on a heavy platform near the helicopter pad.

"Can you see Starsweep coming in yet Rick?" Jason asked.

Without looking away from the eyepiece Rick said, "No, but when the time comes these babies will give us a great view of the action." He swung the giant set of binoculars around so they were aiming at Jo and Jason, jumped back from them and yelled, "Yikes!"

As a group of officers approached, they realized the recovery team leader, Mike Watson, was with them.

Mike said, "Welcome aboard folks! We have a seventy-two hour cruise ahead of us and it looks like everything's in order. Are you ready to set sail?"

With a gruff voice, Jason saluted Mike and said, "Aye, Aye Captain! We're ready to set sail for the high seas and bring the Starsweep back to port."

Mike said, "Clowning aside, I'd like all of you to meet Captain James Blane." As they each extend a handshake greeting, Mike introduced them. "Captain Blane, this is Doctor Jo Kendesh, Rick Johnson and Jason Taylor."

The captain then said, "My pleasure, and welcome aboard the naval cruiser Goddard. With Mike's help, we plan to make this a flawless recovery. If there's anything the Navy can do to further assist you, just let me know. You're welcome to join me in the control tower as we leave port."

Jo replied, "Thank you Captain. We're all looking forward to bringing the Starsweep back home, and from what we hear we're in very capable hands."

"Then let's be on our way to the control tower." Captain Blane turned and walked briskly with his support staff, and the NASA scientists followed closely behind.

As they ascended three flights of stairs to the tower they heard orders being called out in the distance as the docking lines were cast off the ship. The captain gave orders to proceed from port and the large ship began to move toward the channel leading out to sea.

Two armed ships joined the Goddard, one running off the port and one off the starboard side. A fourth communications ship was running directly behind the Goddard. The ocean was calm as they glided through the blue waters of the Pacific, toward the slowly setting sun.

The other ships joining the Goddard on the recovery journey were the cruisers USS San Diego, the USS Kitty Hawk, and the USS Satcom.

The Kitty Hawk and San Diego will patrol the area where the Starsweep will be picked up, while the Satcom will monitor the probe re-entry, and coordinate its tracking with several observatories and satellites around the world.

There would also be added air support from the coast guard based in Hawaii, in case the recovery helicopter needs assistance.

As the small fleet navigated their way southwest that evening, Jo, Rick and Jason arranged to meet Mike on the observation deck of the Goddard. They hoped to spend some time marveling at the night sky over the Pacific. There was no cloud cover to speak of, and the moon was only a sliver in the heavens. It would be a perfect night to see the constellations and the faint glow of the Milky Way. A warm breeze out of the south added to the magic of their journey.

About a mile from each side of the Goddard were the Navy escort ships, and the communication ship followed about a mile behind. This meant no light pollution blocked their spectacular view of the stars.

Occasionally with their bare eyes, they would see a satellite and follow its unmistakable path crossing the night sky. The churning sounds of the ship gliding through the water could be heard in the background, mixed with various intercom calls. They each scanned the horizon in silent wonder, taking in the peaceful awe of nature beneath the starlight from above.

Mike broke the silence among the group as he pointed to the northwest and said, "Look! Just off the bow of the San Diego, a pod of whales is breaking the surface. See their spouts?"

Rick said, "Wow, that's amazing! How many are there?"

Jason scanned the water surface with a small pair of binoculars and said, "I count five or six." Handing them to Jo he said, "Here, how many do you see?" Jo scanned the area for a minute and said, "At least six, maybe seven. It's hard to tell from this distance and in this light. I bet the crew of the San Diego is having fun with a closer view." Mike added, "I'm sure their night watch is keeping an eye on them, but it's not an uncommon sight, so I doubt they're getting too excited."

Handing the binoculars back to Jason, Jo asked, "Isn't it supposed to be good luck to have whales or dolphins travel with a ship?"

Mike responded, "Sounds good to me. We'll take all the luck we can get. Reports are that we may run into some rough weather during splashdown, so let's hope nature holds off on getting irritable until we've picked up the probe. Tomorrow we'll discuss the recovery timeline, and what Plan B is if the weather doesn't cooperate. It's been a long day, so I'm going to turn in. We'll be in the splashdown area the day after tomorrow, and we'll be there sooner than you think."

"Thanks Mike. Good night," Jo replied.

"See you in the morning Mike," Rick added.

Jason raised the binoculars back to his eyes and said, "I'm going to watch our whale friends a little while longer. I'll see you in the morning."

Jo, Rick and Mike each retired to their quarters for the night.

The next morning the seas were heavier, and the rolling waves occasionally threw spray across the deck of the Goddard. The escort ships were still in formation as they continued moving toward the splashdown area.

The skies were clear to partly cloudy, but the winds had picked up enough for the team to realize something could be brewing in the weather over the horizon.

Mike left a message for each member of Jo's observation team saying Captain Blane wanted to meet with them after breakfast. Jo did not have to use any of her seasickness medicine to this point, but she only ate a little breakfast, just to be safe. The rolling sea was making her a bit woozy and she didn't want to push her luck by eating too much.

In fact, everyone at the breakfast table was pretty quiet as they watched the contents of their juice glasses sway back and forth with every rolling wave the ship slid past.

The captain approached their table and said, "Good morning folks! I trust you had a restful night?"

Jo, Rick, Jason and Mike all looked up at the captain with different unsure expressions.

"Our weather reports say we may be in for some rough seas when the Starsweep splashes down, so we'll need to be on alert. The helicopter pick up, which is 300 miles southwest of Hilo, shouldn't be a problem. However, landing the chopper back on the ship's deck could be dangerous, so we will need to move the ship to calmer water before we can land the aircraft. If the weather gets too rough we may need to tow the probe to calm water. By this afternoon we should have a better idea what's in store for us."

Just as Captain Blane finished speaking, Rick tried to take a sip of coffee, and with a lurch of the ship ended up wearing it in his lap.

Mike couldn't help but smile at Rick's mishap, and asked, "Are we havin' fun yet?"

In an attempt to be cool and not admit defeat, Rick stayed calm, carefully poured himself another cup, and brought it back up to his lips. Once again, the ship bounced and Rick had a second helping of hot coffee splashing over his face. At this, everyone at the table burst out laughing while Rick said, "We're havin' fun now!"

Trying to contain his amusement the captain said, "Welcome to the world of the U.S. Navy Mr. Johnson. After you've had a chance to get into some dry clothes, I'd like to meet with your team in the conference room."

While Rick sopped up the mess he asked, "Will you be serving coffee? I haven't had any yet, and I get cranky if I don't have a cup in the morning."

Everyone laughed out loud and agreed to get back together in 45 minutes.

Rick headed for the door last so there was less chance of anyone seeing the large wet spot covering the front of his trousers. Jo figured this would be the case so she waited for him out in the hall.

As he came through the doorway she startled him from behind saying, "Smooth move Archimedes."

Rick's face turned red while he brushed on the wet spot and replied, "Damn waves! If they can stabilize the image on a bouncing video camera, why can't they stabilize something the size of this ship?"

In a matter-of-fact but playful tone Jo stated, "You're just mad, because you wasted a good cup of coffee. Who cares that it made you look like you peed your pants? I'll see you in a bit. I'm going to go take some motion sickness medicine before I end up embarrassing myself too."

As the group began to reassemble in the conference room it was evident the wave motion had picked up. No storm clouds were on the horizon but the rolling waves could no doubt become a concern.

Captain Blane addressed the group once everyone was seated.

"Well folks, as you can probably tell from the motion of our ship, we're going to be working in some rough water during splashdown tomorrow. These waves are being caused by a storm far to the west of our target site. The good news is there's no rain or lightning expected during the recovery operation. The bad news is the sea will be rough enough that we can't safely land the recovery helicopter back on deck once the Starsweep has been picked up. This leaves us two options for recovery.

One is to have the chopper recover the probe and fly southeast about forty-five miles to calmer water. Our ships would then go that way to meet up with it about three hours after the probe is picked up.

The biggest risk with this option is the aircraft could run low on fuel before we get into calm enough water to let her land.

Another option would be to have the recovery helicopter attach a tow cable to the probe, then anchor the other end to the ship. We could then tow the probe toward calmer seas before we hoist it on board. Sort of like reeling in a big fish once you finally catch it.

This option reduces the risk of losing the probe due to the hazards of flight, but we're not sure how the probe would hold up to being towed through high seas for several hours.

That's where having the NASA team aboard is a good thing, since they can tell us which option would be safest."

Mike asked, "Captain, would another option be to let the Starsweep float like a buoy until the high seas pass?"

"It might Mike, if you're confident the Starsweep's float system and locator signal will hold up until the rough seas diminish. If the float system fails, we could end up watching your craft sink to the bottom like a rock. The Pacific basin's about three miles deep in that area, and if we wait until things calm down there is a risk of losing it altogether. Since your craft's only the size of a large sofa it would be nearly impossible to recover from the bottom. We don't have a submarine in the area that can go that deep, so if Starsweep sinks our odds of recovery will be slim."

Mike looked at Jo and asked, "Can the Starsweep handle being towed through rough seas like that?"

She responded, "If the heat shields hold up during re-entry there shouldn't be a problem. If the structure is weakened from too much heat, it's hard to tell how it would react to being pulled through the water like a torpedo for very long. We would almost be forced to cut the floats loose so they don't add too much drag. Then we run the risk of the tow line breaking and the Starsweep sinking."

Rick and Jason both look at each other with worried looks before Rick spoke up.

"Our sample material is housed in a sealed vessel built to withstand the vacuum of space, not the pressure on the ocean floor three miles down!

If the probe sinks to those depths it will be crushed like an empty pop can, and the samples will be destroyed. If the sample material gets contaminated with seawater we will never know the true chemical makeup of the comet. Letting it sink is not an option!"

Jo stood and said, "We agree Rick. We're here to bring the Starsweep back intact. Nobody wants to lose it, especially when it is this close to home!"

Turning to the captain she questioned, "Can your helicopter simply fly the probe to Pearl Harbor after the probe is picked up?"

He replied, "Unfortunately, the chopper doesn't have enough fuel range for that, with the added weight of the probe."

Mike interrupted, "Captain Blane, could we send one of the other ships to calmer water right now? If the helicopter has enough range, tomorrow it could do the pick up as planned, and then fly southeast to put the probe on the other ship in calm water without having to wait for us to get down there."

Captain Blane paused in thought for a moment, and then said, "That might work Mike. Our helicopter has no place to land on the other ships in this group, but it might have enough fuel to do the pick up, fly the probe to calmer seas, lower it by cable to be secured on deck, then head back to Hawaii to land and refuel.

We can arrange to have a Coast Guard plane come out and escort the chopper back to land."

The ship's captain looked at the chopper pilot and asked, "Think this will work?"

The pilot responded, "Hovering during the recovery hookup and flying with the weight of the probe burns the most fuel. If all goes smoothly we might just be able to get to Hilo."

Mike said, "This sounds like our best option Captain. Delivering the probe by cable to the deck of a cruiser will be risky, but the bigger issue will be getting the chopper back to land before it runs out of fuel.

NASA doesn't have a Navy helicopter in the budget for this project and we don't want to put the flight crew in harm's way either."

Captain Blane walked to a north-facing window where the San Diego was visible cutting through the waves in the distance.

He turned to the group and said, "This evening the San Diego will be sent to calmer water. The NASA observation team will be transferred to the San Diego as well. The team will want to inspect the probe once it's on board and if any special handling is necessary, you will need to be present.

After the probe has been picked up it will be delivered to the San Diego. If the Goddard can't get to calm enough water for the chopper to land, it will head directly for the Hawaiian Islands. Our friends in the Coast Guard will provide a fixed wing escort for the chopper while it flies toward the island.

This operation will get the Starsweep probe, and everyone involved with the recovery, home safe and sound. If there are no questions ---- we've got a lot of work to do, so let's get to it!"

As the room emptied, Mike, Jo, Jason and Rick stayed behind to get the details on being transferred to the San Diego.

Captain Blane turned to the group and said, "In about an hour, you NASA observers will need to report to our transport boat launch. You should bring your gear along since the initial inspection and transport back to the mainland will be taking place on the San Diego. Mike, we'll need you to stay on the Goddard and monitor the splashdown recovery."

"Are you confident this will work Captain?" Jo asked.

"We're going to make it work," the captain replied.

Mike added, "This really shouldn't be a problem, but we need to keep moving to make it happen. Starsweep gets closer by the minute and we want to be ready for it. Let's meet at the transport launch as soon as possible, and we'll get over to the San Diego to head for calmer waters."

Mike waited at the transport bay as the ship's crew made final preparations to lower the shuttlecraft to the waves below. Jo, Jason, and Rick arrived one by one wearing windbreakers and carrying duffel bags over their shoulders.

The blowing wind and ocean spray forced Mike to shout at Jo, "The captain has arranged for your accommodations on the San Diego. Once on board you will begin to sail southeast. We'll use radio and video contact during the pick-up and delivery phase of the mission."

Jo shouted back over the swirling wind, "Thanks Mike, I'll contact you once we're settled in!"

Rick and Jason had already boarded the shuttle boat, so Jo tightened her hold on the duffel bag and turned into the wind to climb aboard.

The transfer craft wasn't a small boat, but as it worked its way toward the San Diego the waves created a roller coaster effect. Jo thought to herself that if she hadn't taken her motion sickness medicine earlier she'd be in real trouble right now.

Fortunately, as the shuttle boat moved closer to the San Diego, the ship provided some shelter on the down-wind side where the transfer boat would unload.

The NASA team was amazed how smoothly the Navy crew worked together to bring the shuttle boat in safely.

They each hopped onto the San Diego and were greeted by a short, stocky officer who threw them a salute while shouting, "Welcome aboard the cruiser San Diego! Let's get in out of this wind and I'll show you to your quarters."

Jo, Rick and Jason all nodded and followed their greeter. Once they got inside out of the howling wind the officer led them to a briefing room.

"Please have a seat. I'm Captain Ron Lister, and you're now guests on board the USS San Diego."

"It's a pleasure to meet you Captain, I'm Jo Kendesh. This is Rick Johnson, and Jason Taylor," she announced as she pointed toward each of them. "Can you give us a rundown of what we should expect next?"

The captain replied, "Certainly. As you're well aware, these waves have changed our mission plans. The captains of this four-ship recovery fleet have agreed to send us into smoother seas so the recovery helicopter can deliver the space probe to a level deck. We shouldn't be separated from the fleet for an extended period, but this is believed to be our safest course of action. Tomorrow morning the Starsweep probe will be coming down in rough water, and I have every confidence that Captain Blane's crew will bring the probe to us intact."

Jason asked, "Will we be alone in the area we're headed for?"

"Actually Mr. Taylor, on the surface that will be true, but one of our subs is in the area, so if there is an emergency you can rest assured we're not alone.

If the media plans to cover any of this with their own boats tomorrow, they won't know about this trip until it's already happened."

Rick looked at Jo and Jason and said, "Gee, this should add a touch of covert adventure for your media exposure work, Jo."

Jo replied, "The way these big ships are being tossed around in these waves, I can't imagine a media charter would have much fun trying to follow the recovery in the waters where the Goddard will be located."

The captain added, "Sometimes we're surprised at what resources the media finds to follow this kind of thing."

Rick said, "This mission hasn't had a lot of glamorous hype. A little excitement during recovery due to weather might be interesting to them if it's a slow news day."

"In any case, we'll be patiently waiting in calmer seas while the Goddard crew does their part."

While they were talking, a junior officer had entered the room and was waiting patiently by the door.

The captain said, "This gentleman will give you a quick tour while your bags are being taken to your quarters. Things are set up in the communication tower so we can follow our mission progress during splashdown."

Jo asked, "Where and how will the Starsweep be secured once the helicopter makes its delivery?"

Captain Lister turned to the officer by the door with a look of anticipation and the officer said, "It turns out your probe isn't all that different in size and weight from some of our missiles. As we speak, the crew is in the process of modifying one of our maintenance cradles to hold the Starsweep. This will closely match what the Goddard was going to use in the first place."

With a pleased smile on his face Rick said, "It sure sounds like the Navy has everything covered."

As the captain walked toward the door he said, "We pride ourselves in being ready to react to whatever a situation calls for Mr. Johnson. Once the probe is safely on board, it will be taken below deck to an inspection bay that we are clearing for your use.

If there's anything we can do to assist you once the probe is on board, just let us know."

Jo looked at Rick and Jason to say, "After we've had a chance to freshen up and take a tour let's meet in the communications tower."

Rick replied, "Let's do it!"

They collected their things and made their way to the door. After getting settled in and reassembling in the control tower, Jo made a call on a speakerphone to Mike Watson back on the USS Goddard.

"Hello Mike. Rick, Jason and I are getting oriented on the San Diego. How are things going on the Goddard?"

Mike responded, "Hi Jo. The seas here are as rough as ever, and as we continue southwest it seems to be getting worse. Weather reports say the waves are growing due to the tropical storm. Hopefully things won't get any worse before splashdown."

"I copy that Mike," Jo replied. "As we head southeast things are calming down. How are things going with the Starsweep's approach?"

"Everything looks good. The tracking group tells me splashdown will be around 9:00 A.M. As the probe comes in, we plan to position the Goddard about three miles from the splash site. The chopper crew is ready to fly as soon they get the go signal."

Jason leaned toward the speaker and chimed in, "Hi Mike, this is Jason. Does it look like any other visitors will be in the area to observe the recovery?"

Mike replied, "Interesting you should ask. There's a group of foreign fishing vessels trying to stay ahead of the storm, so they may be off in the distance during recovery. We're warning them to stay clear of the splashdown zone. There aren't any private craft or media vessels trying to brave these waves so it doesn't look like we'll have a big audience."

Jo added, "That's just as well Mike. Since we've had to make last minute changes in how the recovery takes place, we won't need to explain what's going on to a bunch of bystanders."

From the background Rick shouted, "Hey Mike, I'm finally able to have a cup of coffee without throwing it in my lap!"

With a chuckle Mike responded, "Have one for me Rick. We'll be back in touch before the probe comes down in the morning. Try to get some rest, and I'll talk with you later."

Jo said, "Thanks Mike, you get some rest too. We'll be waiting to hear from you."

As they hung up the captain handed Jo a note saying, "This just came in for you."

She read the message and said, "It's a note from IBC asking me to contact them. How did they know where to find me?" Jo asked.

Looking over her shoulder at the note Rick commented, "The media can be a scary bunch."

Still looking at the note Jo scrunched her eyebrows and said, "That's for sure. Somehow they had to know what's happened in the past few hours to track me here. I'll ask Mike if he knows anything about it in the morning."

The next morning Jo awoke to find the water around the San Diego to be quite calm compared to what they sailed out of the evening before.

She got up, got dressed and went directly to the communication tower.

Rick and Jason were already there, looking at radar images while munching on donuts. Jason looked up and greeted Jo while still chewing, "Mornin' Jo, it's finally homecoming day for Starsweep!"

"Good morning guys, how do things look in the splashdown area?"

Rick replied, "Winds are 30 to 40 miles per hour and they're getting gusts up to 50. Not good!"

"Damn, and it's so nice here. Have you talked to Mike yet this morning?" Jo asked.

"We'll be in contact again in forty-five minutes. The Navy divers will have their hands full getting the probe hooked up to the helicopter, but they're saying it can be done."

Jo noticed Captain Lister across the room on the phone. After he hung up, he turned to approach the group.

He greeted them by saying, "Good morning Doctor Kendesh, gentlemen, the probe is on schedule for re-entry but the tracking team can't be certain where it will drift when the parachutes open to slow the craft.

All we can do is monitor the situation and wait until our helicopter makes its delivery.

Everything here is ready to receive the probe and secure it for your inspection."

Jo responded, "Thanks Captain. We're used to waiting for things, but I have to tell you this is about the highest level of anticipation and anxiety I've ever had."

Rick asked, "Is a Coast Guard plane still coming out to follow the chopper back from here to Hawaii?"

"It's in the air as we speak Mr. Johnson. Our pilots are among the best in the world, but they can't keep an aircraft flying without fuel. Let's hope the probe doesn't drift too far off course in the wind and delay our delivery."

An officer approached the captain to inform him he has a conference call coming in with the other recovery fleet captains.

Captain Lister turned to the NASA team and said, "You'll have to excuse me. I'll keep you posted." He then left the room.

Rick started chewing on a pencil as he gazed at the radar monitor. He stopped to look at the pencil. With a sour look on his face he looked up at Jo and said, "Someone should flavor these things." Jo and Jason looked at each other and just shook their heads.

The phone in front of Rick rang and he quickly picked it up.

"Hello? Hi Mike, what's the latest? Wait, let me put you on the speaker." With the push of a button, Jo and Jason could hear Mike's voice.

Rick prompted, "Okay Mike, go ahead."

"They're moving us northeast a few miles to adjust for where they think the wind will push the probe."

Jason asked, "Where did those fishing boats end up?"

Mike responded, "They seem to be headed for the same area you're in. Trying to get out of these waves I'd guess."

Jo picked up a pair of binoculars from a nearby table and moved to a large window. While scanning the horizon she said, "I see four small boats in the distance Mike. Do we know who they are and what they're up to?"

"They appear to be Russian fishing boats. The Navy's keeping an eye on their movement."

"Can they hear our communications?" Jo asked.

"This is supposed to be a secure link Jo. Anyone trying to listen in should be hearing nothing but an electronic scramble. We're not on a secret mission, but no one else needs to know when and why the Navy moves its ships."

"How much time until splashdown Mike?"

"They're now predicting the probe will hit the water about 9:30. It's almost 9:00 now, so it won't be long. It should become visible around ten after. We've arranged to have a video signal sent to you when we can see it."

The NASA team hadn't been paying much attention to activity elsewhere in the room, but just as Mike was sharing this information Jo noticed two crewmen setting up a video monitor on a wheeled cart.

When they turned the monitor on, a view from the helicopter pad on the Goddard became visible.

"No sooner said than done Mike. We're looking at a view from near the helicopter now."

Mike responded, "Remember the huge binoculars on the stand by the chopper? That's where the camera is. I'm going that way now, so you'll see me there in a few minutes. This communication link will stay open throughout the recovery so hang on the line. I'll be back with you in a few minutes."

While they waited for Mike to appear on the video monitor they watched as the helicopter crew made preparations for takeoff. Gear was being loaded on the helicopter while Navy divers climbed aboard.

They noticed the aircraft was still lashed down securely to the pad, so there would be no risk of it being washed overboard. Prior to take off, the engines would be wound up so the rotor blades could create plenty of lift before the craft is let go. When the signal is given, the cables will be released and the chopper will immediately lift off. This system works well for rough weather takeoffs, but it's a one-way process. Once the cables are released there is no turning back.

Soon Mike appeared on the video monitor wearing a set of headphones. He waved at the camera and said, "Hi guys, it won't be long and the Starsweep will be visible as a bright spot in the western sky. The parachutes will be the first things visible. We'll focus the camera on the probe and try to follow it all the way to the water. Once it lands, the chopper will take off, pick up the craft, and start heading your way. I can hear you through these headphones, so if you have comments or questions just speak up."

Rick said, "This is great Mike! I don't care what others may say, your recovery team is a class act."

No sooner had Rick finished with his back handed compliment, when the camera zoomed toward the clouds and a cluster of three small white dots became visible.

Mike stated, "With a strong zoom we can see the drag chutes now. Can you guys see it?"

With excitement in her voice Jo shouted, "We can see it Mike, we can see it!"

In the background the helicopter engines could be heard starting to warm up. The white canopies of three parachutes became clearer in the picture as they drifted in and out of sight through the high cloud cover.

The wave motion of the ship was still very evident, with wind driven spray washing over the deck. This reminded them why they were on the San Diego in calm water, and the other ships were several miles away.

With a laugh in his voice Jason said, "Have them hold the camera still Mike, we keep losing our view of the probe with all that bouncing around."

A brief response came back, "You're a funny guy Taylor. Wish you were here."

Jason and Rick looked at each other and raised their eyebrows in surprise, since Mike usually took their ribbing with good humor.

As the probe got closer to the water, the helicopter engines could be heard increasing in speed as it prepared to leave the flight deck.

The Starsweep was drifting with the wind to the northeast of the Goddard. Everyone knew the farther it went that direction the farther the helicopter would have to go to deliver the probe and get back to land without running out of fuel. The tension mounted by the minute as the probe got closer to the rolling waves of the ocean surface.

It seemed like it took forever for the probe to come down before it was lost on the camera behind a large swell. The parachute lines could be seen going somewhat limp above the waves but no splash was visible from the probe hitting the water.

Almost at the same instant, the helicopter engines reached their highest pitch, and the tie down cables could be heard releasing like bullwhips cracking in the distance.

The camera zoomed back to follow the helicopter moving up and away from the Goddard. It immediately banked steeply in the direction of the spacecraft and seemed like an Olympic sprinter bursting away from the blocks at the sound of the starter's pistol.

There was a strange silence over the communication link once the engine noise faded into the wind. No one spoke. All eyes were on the monitor as the camera followed the helicopter toward the splashdown site. The parachutes had quickly settled into the water, and only brief glimpses of their white material could be seen on the surface between the huge waves surrounding the probe.

A voice came over the link from the helicopter saying, "Goddard this is Sky Hook, we've run into a problem. The chutes didn't release when the probe hit the water. It looks like four floats inflated properly, but the divers will have to try and cut the chutes loose before we can hook up and transport."

Jo looked at Rick and Jason and said, "Not good. Every minute they have to monkey with cutting those chutes loose, is a minute less fuel they'll have."

Rick added, "Trying to cut those lines on dry land would be tough, I can't imagine doing it in those waves."

Looking at the monitor Jo asked, "What will they do Mike?"

After a brief pause, Mike responded, "The Navy divers carry magnesium torches. They look kind of like road flares, but they burn under water and can cut through steel, so cutting the lines shouldn't be a problem. A bigger risk will be popping the floats, or cutting into the Starsweep itself, while they're fighting these waves, and the clock!"

The camera stayed zoomed in on the splashdown site, and to their horror they could see where there once were four floats surrounding the probe, there were now only three.

Over the communication link they hear, "Goddard, they're cutting lines but we've lost a float. How many will still keep the probe on top?"

Mike jumped in front of the camera, which immediately refocused on him.

"What do you think Jo?"

She responded, "Two should keep it buoyant, but in these waves I'm not sure. In a quiet test tank one float will keep it about 20 feet below the surface. Let's pray we don't lose any more!"

As Mike moved out of the camera's view, it zoomed back to the splashdown site. Now it appeared there were only two floats visible as the probe bobbed up and down between the waves. It also appeared to dip beneath the surface again and again.

Rick asked, "Mike, can they hook the damn probe onto the chopper in case we lose another float?"

Mike replied, "Not until the chute lines are all cut clear. The drag those lines create could pull the aircraft into the water."

They all watched in fear as the divers continued working frantically to free the Starsweep from its parachute lines. The next thing they saw was a line coming down from the helicopter with a diver attached to the end.

It appeared the parachute lines had finally been cut free. The diver on the cable swayed back and forth in the wind, as it got closer to the probe. Those in the water reached to catch him and moved quickly to attach the cable needed to hoist the probe out of the water.

At the same time they watched another line being lowered toward the water. One diver grabbed the second line and one by one the others moved toward him and begin to form a human chain. The line was slowly raised from the water, lifting one, two, three, then four men out of the water toward the helicopter.

Everyone watched breathlessly as the helicopter struggled to hover over the probe and slowly lift the four divers higher and higher above the cresting waves. If the diver line got tangled with the probe line it would be disastrous.

Fortunately, the wind direction was tending to push the diver line away from the probe line. It continued to get closer to the helicopter, and not a word was being spoken by anyone throughout the communication grid.

The diver line finally reached the helicopter and one by one they climbed into the aircraft. The chopper slowly began to lift, and for the first time the Starsweep became visible as it rose out of the water.

Jo shouted, "They have it Mike! They have it!"

He replied, "We're not out of the woods yet Jo, the two floats that are still in place need to be deflated before they can move any distance at any speed. They were supposed to deflate automatically with a signal from the Goddard, but they're not responding. We're open for suggestions on this end."

After a brief silence Mike added, "One of the crew members here suggested they shoot them to deflate."

Jo responded, "No! If they miss they could damage the Starsweep. Let's think of something else."

Suddenly the camera revealed one of the divers tethered to the helicopter, sliding down the cable attached to the probe. When he reached the probe it appeared he began using a sharp object to puncture the floats. One at a time they popped like party balloons. He then began to be pulled back up toward the chopper.

Jason remarked, "Are these guys good or what?"

Rick chuckled, "They're nuts too."

As soon as the diver was pulled into the chopper it began to fly to the southeast at an ever-increasing speed. Soon it faded to a small spot and disappeared from the camera's view.

Mike shouted, "She's headed your way Jo! Let us know when the probe's safely aboard the San Diego! Over and out."

With that, the screen went blank, and Captain Lister entered the room.

"Well folks, the Sky Hook helicopter will be here in about an hour with the Starsweep probe. Our crew is ready to take delivery, so by this afternoon we should be sailing back for California. The Goddard, Kitty Hawk and Satcom are all heading northeast, and we'll regroup tonight to travel back to port together.

The trouble they had cutting the parachutes free cost them precious time and fuel, so when the probe is released, they'll be dropping every bit of extra weight they can before flying to Hawaii."

"What kind of extra weight can they drop?" Jason quizzed.

"The four divers you watched do the hookup, the flight navigator, the copilot and all their gear will be dropped into the ocean."

The only person left on board will be the pilot. If all goes as planned the Starsweep drop can't take more than 15 minutes. Even then, he will be running on fumes by the time he reaches land.

A Coast Guard rescue plane has already caught up with the chopper and will stay with him until he gets back. If the 'copter runs out of fuel over water, the plane will drop a life raft and communicate with rescue craft during the pilot's recovery.

By the way, just so you're aware, another interesting development came up during the recovery. We're not so sure the four fishing boats we've been watching on the horizon are what they appear to be.

At this point there's no reason for alarm, but we don't want to take any chances either. In the event that something becomes unsafe, we'll secure you folks with the probe in the inspection bay. Any questions?"

Jo answered, "The Navy has gotten us this far Captain. We trust you'll get us the rest of the way."

With that, Captain Lister said, "Five minutes before the chopper arrives, an alert will be sounded throughout the ship. Report to the deck at mid-ship, and you can watch the Starsweep come aboard."

The captain then turned and left the room.

Jo looked at the donut crumb mess Rick and Jason left on the table and realized she hadn't eaten since last night.

"I'm going to grab something to eat before that alert sounds. Are you guys with me?"

Holding an outstretched arm in the direction of the door Jason said, "Lead the way Doctor Kendesh."

As the three NASA team members were finishing up their sandwiches in the ship's mess hall, a repeating buzzer began to sound over the ship's intercom system. Jo looked at her watch, as crewmembers began to run for their assigned stations.

Rick wiped his mouth with a napkin and said, "It's show time folks, let's go watch this baby be delivered."

They all pushed away from the table and rushed to the deck area where the chopper would be arriving.

By the time they got to the receiving area they could hear the helicopter engines in the distance. The captain waved to them from an upper deck railing and yelled, "Join me up here!"

They climbed up a flight of stairs to a platform area where they had a clear view of the helicopter and escort plane approaching.

On deck there was a cradle with a sling that looked like something a national aquarium might use to transport small whales from tank to tank.

A landing raft was already nearby in the water ready to pick up the divers, flight crew and their gear.

As the helicopter got about one-hundred yards from the ship, it dropped to twenty feet above the surface and the side doors slid open. One by one, the divers jumped into the water below. The last two on board threw several bags filled with gear into the water below. The bags briefly sank then floated back to the surface.

They then moved back inside as the chopper slowly approached the ship deck and began lowering the probe. The two crewmen remaining on the helicopter helped guide the pilot and operate the winch to lower the Starsweep onto the cradle. The ship's crew also helped the pilot align the probe with the cradle using hand and radio signals. The captain leaned toward Jo and yelled over the noise of the engines, "This will be a lot easier without the waves!" Jo nodded her head in agreement and continued to watch.

Once the probe was placed in the cradle and strapped down to the ship, the attachment cable was released and drawn back up into the helicopter.

The chopper then moved a short distance from the ship, and after a brief pause, the last two flight-crew members leapt into the water wearing life preservers.

As the pilot threw a salute to everyone on board and in the water, he gained altitude, rotated the craft toward the Hawaiian Islands and moved off into the distance. The escort plane made a wide circle overhead, and followed the chopper toward the horizon.

Crewmen wheeled the Starsweep to an elevator platform where it began to disappear below deck.

Captain Lister turned to Jo and extended his hand in congratulations for the successful return of the space probe. Jo looked down at his hand, hesitated, then threw both arms around him and yelled, "We did it!"

Rick and Jason gave each other high fives and the ship's crew could be heard letting loose a few hoots and hollers in the background.

Chapter 3

What The?

As the freight elevator slowly moved the Starsweep and its attendants toward the lower deck, Rick, Jo and Jason looked with awe at the charred exterior.

This small probe had just returned from traveling millions of miles through the freezing depths of space. The fact that it also survived the heat of re-entry while coming through Earth's atmosphere made its incredible journey even more amazing.

Rick pointed to an area where some of the heat shield tiles had fallen off. Without touching it, he followed the perimeter of the area with his index finger and said, "Look at this."

As Jason looked over another section of the probe he added, "There's more over here. Some of these areas look like tiles were missing during re-entry. Look how the exposed metal appears to have turned molten and then was reshaped as it cooled."

While intently surveying the damaged areas, Jo commented, "Some of this might be from the torches our divers used to cut the parachute lines with. Whatever caused it, let's hope the shielding and seals around our comet material held up so no contamination occurred."

Just then, the elevator came to a stop and two large metal doors opened to reveal a room separating the elevator from the inspection bay.

This entry was set up for equipment cleaning and crew decontamination. Before anyone or anything could enter or leave the clean room, they had to go through this area. There were armed guards stationed by the entry as well. Only authorized personnel were being allowed into the inspection bay area.

The NASA team was impressed by how quickly all this was set up, since the San Diego was not the ship Starsweep was originally supposed to be brought back home on.

As everyone was having their identification badges checked by the guards, a voice came over the intercom system saying, "Will Doctor Kendesh please pick up the nearest com line?"

Jo looked at one of the guards and raised both hands to question where she might find a phone. He pointed to a box hanging on the wall nearby. She opened the cover, picked up the receiver and said, "Hello, this is Jo Kendesh."

A voice responded, "Jo, this is Mike! We're told the Starsweep made it on board the San Diego in one piece, and the helicopter is on its way back to Hawaii. How do things look?"

"Well Mike," she replied, "We're just bringing it into the decontamination area. Soon we'll be in the inspection bay taking a closer look. It appears we lost some of the heat shield tiles, but we don't know if that's caused any problems yet."

Mike responded, "On our way back to California the ships will regroup. The wind and waves are beginning to let up as we travel northeast, so we're looking forward to smoother sailing and your report on how successful the recovery was."

"We'll keep you posted Mike. Thanks again for all your help getting us this far. By the way, I forgot to ask you something during all the recovery excitement. How would anyone at IBC know where to contact me after we transferred to this ship?"

"Good question Jo. I don't think anyone from NASA or the Navy has been telling them our plans. You'll have to ask them yourself. Hey, ask Captain Lister about those fishing boats too. You might be interested to hear what took place while the Starsweep was being dropped off."

"I'll ask him about it Mike. We'll keep you updated on the Starsweep's condition."

Jo hung up, closed the box and hurried to catch up with Jason and Rick.

They were already in the decontamination room taking notes. A member of the crew handed them clean, white cover suits and hoods to put on over their street clothes. The inspection room the Starsweep was in is normally an emergency surgery room. It had its own air filtering system to help ensure a clean environment.

As she put on her cover-suit, the captain approached and addressed Jo.

"Doctor Kendesh, if there's anything my crew can do to help just ask. A team has been assigned to guard the area and assist with whatever you need."

Jo said, "Thanks Captain. The Navy has proven to be a wonder at making things happen in a moment's notice and being very adaptable. You're an amazing bunch.

By the way, Mike Watson said I should ask you about the fishing boats that were in the distance during the recovery. Was there a problem?"

The captain responded, "During the excitement of the helicopter delivering the probe you probably didn't notice our submarine surface in the distance. The foreign boats started to move in too close for comfort.

They stopped dead in their tracks at the sight of a nuclear sub surfacing in front of them. Our subs don't like to surface, since it gives away their presence and position, but it was the only quick way to show them we're not alone out here."

"Weren't they just fishing boats?" Jo asked.

"Fishing for information is probably more like it," the captain remarked. "After about twenty minutes the sub went back under, and the boats started moving southwest as we went our own way."

Jo was still puzzled about being called by IBC after she came aboard the San Diego. With that in mind she asked, "Is there a chance those boats had anything to do with the media? I got a message from the IBC asking me to call, and I can't figure out how they knew we made these last minute plans to board your ship."

"I doubt these boats were with the media," he replied. "At first they were identified as Russian fishing vessels, and we're checking that out with the Russian government. They may just be curious fishermen, but I'd be surprised if that were the case.

It's also possible they were Chinese or North Korean vessels. Our space program has always been a key point of interest for those countries. If they thought we were recovering a spy satellite that would explain their presence."

"Are we in any danger?" Jo asked.

"No. There are no armed naval ships in the area other than our own, and everyone seems to be going their separate ways now. They know we have underwater support and they know they'd be sitting ducks if trouble were to start."

"Thanks for the update Captain. If you'll excuse me now, I have a space ship to inspect."

Jo pulled on the head cover to her cleanroom suit, flipped the clear visor down over her face, and entered the inspection bay.

The discussion with Captain Lister made Jo feel more at ease as she entered the inspection bay where the Starsweep now rested. She still didn't have an answer as to how IBC knew where she was, but there were more important things to concentrate on now.

As Jo moved toward the Starsweep, Rick and Jason motioned for her to come and look at something.

Jason focused a video camera on the probe, while Rick used a laser pointer to highlight various areas of damage.

Rick spoke as the video recorder followed his inspection, "Here we can see an area where heat shield tiles are missing, and the outer shell of the probe is pitted with small craters of various sizes and depths. It's possible that these tiles were lost during the journey around the comet. High-speed impacts with debris in space may have knocked the tiles off, which would have exposed the metal to this kind of pitting and erosion."

Jason ran the camera's zoom back out and focused on Jo. "Now to find out what we've all been waiting for. Did the dust collection chamber remain intact?" They moved around to the side of the probe and carefully inspected the area where the chamber was opened in space to gather comet dust.

The collection chamber was their main area of concern. Once the comet dust was gathered and the chamber door closed, the seal system became permanent until a special cutting operation could be performed back at their lab.

The design actually used the heat of re-entry to help weld the door seal shut. No open seams or gaps were evident around the dust collection door.

Rick moved the laser pointer around the area of the door perimeter as Jason followed with the video.

Jo announced, "The chamber door seal appears to be in good condition, so when we get back to the lab in Houston we expect the sample material to be free of contamination."

Jason paned the video image back, so Jo was visible in the picture. She then gave the thumbs up sign.

They continued to scan the Starsweep, taking notes and trying to determine what caused different types of damage, and when it might have occurred.

When they were finished, they set up a tripod and took some playful portrait-style pictures of themselves with the probe in the background.

Though the craft appeared to be intact, the clean room environment would be maintained for the rest of their journey as a precaution.

Jo said, "Let's share what we've seen here with Mike and the others, and find out how our helicopter is doing."

Back in the ship's communication tower, Captain Lister relayed some good news with the recovery team. He said the helicopter landed safely at Hilo, but it was dangerously low on fuel. Though there were problems with the water recovery, the probe delivery went smoothly and quickly on the San Diego, and the chopper pilot made it back to land safely.

The Goddard, Kitty Hawk and Satcom were all in the process of regrouping with the San Diego. During their journey back, the San Diego would be front and center in formation, since it was carrying the Starsweep.

Once they were back at port in California, the probe would be transported to the NASA lab in Houston, so study of the Johnson-Taylor Comet material could begin.

Jo decided it might be a good time to call her IBC contact and share the news of the successful recovery.

She still had reporter Susan McCalum's number in her cell phone directory, so she auto-dialed.

The phone rang twice and Susan answered, "IBC, this is Susan."

"Hello Susan, this is Jo Kendesh with NASA."

"Jo! Thanks for calling back! How did things go with your comet probe recovery?"

"It went well. We're on our way back to Houston to begin studying what the probe picked up. Say, can I ask you a question?"

"Sure Jo, what is it?" Susan replied.

"How did you know where I was during the recovery?"

"Well, some commercial space technology helped us there. The distance, the weather in the Pacific, and our budget didn't allow us to follow the recovery in person, so the network hired a private satellite imaging service.

It's amazing how clearly we were able to follow the recovery ship movements. When we noticed a shuttle moving between ships, followed by a ship heading toward calmer water we took a guess that rough seas meant your recovery plans had changed. If the probe was being brought to calm water, you would probably be going there too."

"Good Lord Susan! It sounds like you folks should work for the CIA!"

Susan laughed and said, "Our budget isn't that big Jo. We can't afford to be that inefficient either. Now that I've shared one of our secrets, what can you share about yours?"

"Excuse me?" Jo replied.

"The satellite watched four boats turn away after what looked like a submarine appeared. Is there more to studying comet dust than you're sharing?"

"Not at all Susan. I was told those were fishing boats, and they just got a little too close. I hope you're not thinking of making up a story just to increase viewer interest."

"I won't if you won't Jo. Keep in touch on your discoveries, and I think we can help each other out. You get more exposure campaigning for project support and funds, while we get the latest breaking news on your discoveries. Can we work something out?"

"I don't know Susan, I'm not very comfortable with what I'm hearing."

"Think about it Jo. We're not into making up news to raise ratings, but we like to make news alliances that can give us an edge in the business. We prefer to get stories straight from a source rather than speculating on what satellite pictures might show."

"Susan, let me get back to you when I return to Houston. At this point all I can say is the probe looks to be intact, and we're looking forward to learning more about what a deep space visitor like the Johnson-Taylor Comet is made of."

"Okay, thanks Jo. Meanwhile, think about our discussion."

The line disconnected, and Jo slowly hung up on her end.

Jason asked, "What's wrong Jo, you look upset. Motion sickness catching up with you again?"

"No, but it feels about the same. Apparently our media friends took a guess where I was by following our ship movements with commercial satellite imaging."

Rick said to Jo, "Didn't Captain Blane of the Goddard say he was amazed how resourceful the media can be sometimes?"

Then with a sly tone in his voice Rick added, "Maybe your media friend is a spy."

Jo replied, "Spy shmy! If anyone tries to turn our hard work into a circus just to boost their ratings I'll be a little more than upset."

Jason came back with, "Come on Jo, lighten up. Rick's right. Maybe a little international intrigue is just what we need to spice up the deep space program image. Everyone likes a good mystery."

The return trip to harbor in California seemed to take forever, as did the flight back to Houston. Jo could not stop thinking about what they might find while studying the comet material.

Back in the NASA lab, the Starsweep was once again in a clean room environment, and the scientists were prepared to cut through the main collection chamber seal.

Once this door was opened they would find a smaller container inside, about the size of a thirty- gallon waste canister. This canister had its own special seal, and the comet dust was inside this vessel. It would be taken out of the Starsweep and put into a large inspection box, which was made of two-inch thick glass.

This box had several scientific instruments inside that would help test the comet material properties. It was also equipped with several sets of arm-length gloves. This feature allowed the scientists to work with the material from outside the box, while the dust remained isolated inside. It also kept the scientists from coming in direct contact with their samples from outer space.

Special care was taken to protect the comet material from being exposed to the Earth's atmosphere.

Before the final seal was broken and the dust container opened, all the air in the inspection box would be removed, and replaced with helium. This would prevent the comet dust from being contaminated by pollutants, or reactive gasses in the air we breathe, like oxygen.

Once everything was in order, Jo gave the signal to cut the main door seal open.

A NASA technician began using a special saw that worked a little like the saw a doctor uses to remove a plaster cast from a broken arm or leg. To keep the area clean and chip free, the saw had a vacuum hose positioned near the cutter, and cooling fluid was sprayed on the cutting tool. The vacuum sucked up all the debris as Starsweep's door seal was carefully removed.

Everyone watched intently as the cutter slowly moved around the door edges. After what seemed an eternity the door seal broke free.

As the door opened, the dust collection canister became visible. A pair of large stainless steel tongs mounted on a floor hoist was used to reach into the probe and grab the canister.

The canister was carefully removed from the probe, and then slowly placed in the glass inspection box. Next, the inspection box door closed, and automatic clamps sealed it shut.

Vacuum pumps started to remove the air from the box as it was being filled with helium at the same time. This process would take several hours, so Jo, Rick, and Jason used the time to inspect and document the condition of the probe's interior.

During the inspection, they paid close attention to areas where heat shield tiles had been damaged or had fallen off. They also saw areas where the metal casing had become extremely thin.

Jo commented, "From what we're seeing, it wouldn't have taken much more pressure to break through the probe walls in some places. It's a good thing we chose not to try and drag Starsweep to calm water. It looks like it might have filled with water and possibly contaminated the comet samples."

Rick remarked, "Water inside wouldn't have been a problem as long as the seals on the collection canister stayed intact. We're still lucky things held together. Our comet material should be just the way it was when it was scooped up in space.

Let's go grab a bite to eat and come back when the inspection chamber is finished filling with helium."

Later that evening, their moment-of-truth arrived as they returned to the lab to open the collection canister.

Based on the data Starsweep was sending back throughout the mission, they already felt they had an idea about what they might find.

Unfortunately, some things cannot be learned from a spectrometer in space. This instrument only gave indications of the comet's base elements. It could not show them the structures, chemistry or age of the material.

Their excitement was mounting. Rick and Jason checked the helium level in the chamber and told Jo it looked good. It would now be safe to open the canister.

Jason operated a robotic arm that slowly clamped to the top of the collection container. As it rotated counter-clockwise a hissing sound could be heard as the vacuum inside was released. This also meant the canister was filling with helium from inside the inspection box.

Everyone looked at each other with anticipation as the lid was set aside.

The comet dust had been collected in a bed of material known as aerogel, which is an incredibly lightweight material. The best way to visualize it is to imagine smoke that has turned to a fluffy solid. Thousands of times lighter than cotton, it was the perfect cushion to act like a catcher's mitt for dust in space.

As they looked down into the canister, they could see the aerogel that once filled the cavity to the top had been crushed down to about one-third its original size. This was a good sign, since it could only mean there had been a considerable amount of comet material collected. The aerogel could be easily separated from the comet dust. It added very little weight and took up almost no space. In fact, from weighing the canister now and comparing the current weight to what the canister weighed when it was launched, they knew they had collected nearly three ounces of comet dust.

Jo reached into the canister holding a small metal scoop in her glove-covered hand. While looking through the inspection box glass, she scooped some of the material up and lifted it out of the canister.

As the scoop came into view, their first impression was that the material had the appearance of gray and white campfire ash.

Jo shook a small amount of it onto a glass slide and put it under a video microscope lens, then put the rest of what she had scooped up into the holding tray of a materials analyzer.

Everyone in the room could see the large, flat display of the video microscope. It came into focus at 10X magnification and right away Jason had a puzzled look on his face.

In all his years of studying geology, including Earth rock forms, lunar rocks, and meteorite material, he had never seen a structure like this before.

He asked, "Is the scope working right Jo?"

"It all checks out Jason. I'll go to higher magnification," she replied.

This didn't help. The more she zoomed in, the more complex the material looked.

"What does the analyzer say it's made of?" Rick asked.

Studying a computer screen that showed a plot of various elements and concentrations Jo said, "This is really strange guys. We're looking at an odd mix of crystalline, and inorganic material that the NASA database can't identify."

While still staring at the video screen Rick exclaimed, "Cool! Who would have thought we'd find something new right off the bat?"

Jo turned her attention to the material analyzer. This machine used different non-destructive test methods to determine what elements were present.

She shared what the machine was showing with Rick and Jason, as they continued to puzzle over the microscope screen.

"There doesn't appear to be any new elements here, but we're certainly looking at an unknown structure. This stuff had to be exposed to some unique conditions to cause this."

"Maybe extreme radiation exposure with pressure and temperature cycling?"

Jason suggested, "Let's run a sample through the solvent analyzer. I'm curious if it will break down into something more recognizable."

Jo put a small sample into a separate machine that checks material reactions with various acids, solutions and solvents, with some tests being as simple as mixing the material with fresh water and salt water.

Shortly after she placed the sample in the analyzer it gave her an error message.

"Now what?" she mumbled to herself.

Opening up an inspection plate on the machine she could see what looked like sand in the mechanism.

She said, "What's with this? Wasn't this equipment cleaned and inspected before it was set up?"

Jason responded, "Absolutely. I inspected it all and ran the calibration tests myself. What's the trouble?"

In an annoyed voice Jo fumed, "It looks like it's full of sand!"

Jason and Rick came over to see for themselves, and sure enough, part of the machine had what looked like sand inside the transfer parts.

"That's weird. I know it was clean when I set it up."

Rick told Jo, "Let's put some of what we're looking at into the other analyzer."

Jo gives Rick a look of disgust as though they were going to waste precious time studying a problem with housekeeping, rather than learn more about the comet material.

He noticed her reaction and said, "Humor me."

She brushed some of the granules onto an inspection slide and put it into the other analyzer.

"Just as I thought. It's sand! I don't believe this! Now we have to spend two hours cleaning and readjusting the solvent analyzer before we can go on!"

Jason puts his hands on his hips, turns away from Jo and starts shaking his head from side to side.

Rick spoke up and said, "Look, let's just get it cleaned up and get on with our work. Shit happens, right? We've been pretty darn lucky with how this mission has gone so far, so a little sand won't be the end of the world."

Jo pulled her arms out of the inspection box gloves and said, "You're right. I'm sorry I yelled Jason. Let's just get this thing cleaned up and get on with our work."

While Jo was talking, Jason slowly walked back to the video screen in deep thought.

After Jo finished giving the analyzer a thorough cleaning, she told Rick and Jason they were ready to proceed again.

She again put a small amount of the comet material into the analyzer, and after a few seconds, "ERROR" appeared on the screen again.

Jo exclaimed, "What the?"

Both Rick and Jason were watching over her shoulder as she opened the inspection plate again, and just like before, it appeared that there was sand in the mechanism.

Rick asked, "What phase of the test is this happening in?"

Jo replied, "It's when a small amount of the sample is simply mixed with water!"

Jason looked over at the video microscope display again and in a low tone mumbled, "Oh My God! Is that possible?"

Rick and Jo looked at each other with concern, and then back at Jason.

Jason continued, "Jo, put a small amount of the comet dust on a glass slide. I want to try something."

Jason drew a small amount of bottled drinking water into a hypodermic syringe and placed the syringe in a pass-through chamber that was isolated from the comet material. Partition doors in this compartment allowed items to be moved safely in and out of the main inspection box.

He then put his arms into a set of the inspection gloves and told Jo, "Hand me the sample slide."

She gave the slide with comet dust on it to Jason, and he moved it into the pass-through chamber where the syringe was located.

Jo and Rick were watching Jason's every move without saying a word.

Closing the pass-through chamber doors, Jason moved from the inspection chamber to a set of gloves that reached into the pass-through chamber. He picked up the syringe and slowly pushed a drop of water from the syringe needle onto the comet dust granules resting on the slide.

In the blink of an eye the three scientists saw the water drop turn into what appeared to be several grains of sand.

Rick shouted, "HOLY CRAP!"

Jason looked at Jo to see her eyes fixed on what just happened. A tear welled up and rolled down her cheek.

Without saying a word she looked up at Jason, then over at Rick. Pulling her arms out of the inspection gloves she walked to a nearby chair and sat down. Leaning forward she put her elbows on her knees and her face in her hands.

"Are you okay?" Rick asked.

Slowly she looked up and said, "What would have happened if the Starsweep broke apart in the Pacific?"

Jason responded with a simple, "Wow."

Jo continued, "What if this were to fall into the wrong hands?"

Rick and Jason look at each other, then back at Jo as they began to understand where she was coming from.

In an effort to try and lighten the mood Jason quipped, "We don't know how far this reaction can go Jo, there's probably nothing to really worry about."

She began shaking her head as if to say no, and said, "This material could mean the end of life on Earth. What we just witnessed can't leave this room. I'll meet with our director as soon as possible and find out where we go from here."

Jo walked over to the video microscope, turned off the power and said, "Let's lock it up. I'll call you both in the morning. Remember, not a word to anyone."

Chapter 4

Understanding

During the drive home, Jo called her boss, Ted Preston, the newly appointed director of NASA.

She hated calling him at home, but this was too important to wait until tomorrow. After dialing the phone rang several times and Jo began to get anxious about whether anyone would answer. The line was finally picked up, "Hello?"

"Ted, this is Jo Kendesh, sorry to bother you at home."

"Not a problem Jo, what can I do for you?" he asked.

"We've discovered something about our comet material, and I need to talk with you about it right away."

"Can it wait until tomorrow? I'm preparing for a meeting and I've got a lot of work to do."

"Actually Ted, we need to talk now. Can I stop by your house?"

"What's so important?"

"I can't talk about it on the cell phone Ted, but trust me, this is big."

"Well, okay Jo. When should I expect you?"

"I'll be there in about half an hour."

"Okay, I'll see you soon."

"Thanks Ted."

She disconnected the line, pressed harder on the accelerator and began to pass traffic.

Red flashing lights could be seen ahead as a police car pulled someone over. Jo backed off on her speed to try to avoid the same fate.

As she worked her way through traffic, she thought about what they saw in the lab.

Jo got a sinking feeling as she realized their discovery could not be shared with anyone.

She wondered what would happen to her research now. They still needed to study and understand the structure of the comet material, but now their findings will become top secret.

How would the government cover this up so other scientists around the world don't get suspicious?

Normally after research like this is completed, some of the material is shared with other scientists around the world, to verify research findings. Then material is put on public display in high profile museums, the same way the Apollo moon rocks went on tour.

As Jo pulled into the director's driveway, the porch light came on.

She jumped out of the car and quickly ran to the front door. Before she could knock, the door opened and Ted greeted her, "Hi Jo, come on in. What's this all about?"

"Can we talk alone?" she asked, as she looked around the entry and noticed Ted's kids watching TV in the den.

"Let's go into my study. We'll have more privacy there."

Ted led Jo down a short hall and turned into a small room with books stacked from floor to ceiling. He closed the door behind them and asked, "Now what's this all about?"

Jo responded, "I know this sounds crazy, but we can't release our findings about the material we brought back with Starsweep. In fact, we might be better off figuring out the best way to get rid of it."

"What are you talking about Jo? After all the time and effort spent promoting this mission, you're saying we need to hide or destroy what you've discovered? Why?"

Jo paused, looked at the floor, and then back up at Ted. In a quiet but urgent voice she said, "The comet dust structure is unlike anything we've ever seen. We thought we were having trouble with the solvent analyzer, but it turns out we discovered the dust somehow physically changes water into sand."

"Sand?" Ted shouted.

Jo waved her hands and warned, "Shhhh! I know it's nuts, but we verified the results, and it definitely changes water to silica."

"My God Jo, that's amazing! Do you realize you may have discovered what happened to water on Mars? It might even explain some mysteries here on Earth, too!"

In a disgusted tone she whispered, "Tell me about it. We make one of the most important discoveries in history, and we can't tell anyone."

Ted responded, "Surely we don't have enough material to transform all the water on Earth, do we?"

"We don't know Ted. If it's a chain reaction there might be. Even if there isn't, how long will it be before someone figures out how to copy the structure in a lab to make more? There doesn't appear to be any new elements in the stuff, but everything's arranged in a very new way."

"How so?" Ted asked.

"It has a crystal structure we've never seen before. We're not sure how it formed. Maybe pressure and temperature cycling under extreme radiation?"

"Who else knows about this Jo?"

"Just Rick, Jason, you, and myself," she replied.

"Good. I'll take this to the Security Council in the morning and get back to you. You're right about keeping it under wraps. I want to meet with you, Rick, and Jason at the lab after lunch tomorrow. Leave things locked up until then. Now go home and try to get some rest."

"Yeah, right," Jo groaned.

Ted opened the study door and showed Jo back to the porch. They exchanged waves as she hopped into her car to head for home.

During the drive her cell phone rang and she immediately answered, "Hello?"

"Jo, its Rick. What was Ted's reaction to what we found?"

"This isn't a secure line Rick, so I can't share anything other than he wants to meet with us at the lab after lunch tomorrow. Things will stay locked up until we meet with him."

"Okay Jo. I'll let Jason know, and we'll see you at the lab after lunch."

"Rick, let's be thinking about what something like this could explain. Even though we may never be able to publish any of this, I'd like to collect as many thoughts as possible on what mysteries this could explain in our solar system. Right here on Earth too, for that matter."

"Sure Jo, I'm way ahead of you. I'll bet Jason has some ideas as well. We can go over them tomorrow. Take it easy, and we'll see you at the lab."

"Thanks Rick, have a good night."

Jo hung up and continued to make her way home.

When she arrived, there were three messages on the answering machine. One was from her mother, one was from a local department store with a credit card offer, and the last one was from Susan McCalum at IBC.

Jo said, "That's all we need now, the media poking around for information when we've just discovered such a horrible thing!"

She thought to herself, if I don't call and tell her something she'll get suspicious after the episode with the satellite pictures. I need to wait until tomorrow to call. By then, we will have direction from Ted's meeting with the Security Council.

Jo deleted the credit card ad on the answering machine, then dialed her parent's number.

"Hi, Mom! How are you?"

"Jo! It's good to hear from you! How was your trip?"

"Good Mom. The weather could have been better, but the Starsweep made it back to Earth and we can't wait to start studying the comet samples."

"Are you getting enough sleep?" her mother quizzed.

"No, but that's nothing new. How's Dad?"

"Oh, he's doing fine. He's playing cards at a buddy's place right now, but I'll let him know you're back and that we talked."

"Thanks Mom. Give Dad some hugs and kisses for me, and I'll be in touch."

"Okay dear. Thanks for calling, and be sure to take care of yourself."

"I will Mom. I love you guys. Goodbye."

As she hung up, Jo felt bad that she had to make it sound like everything was fine. Her upbringing made it hard for Jo to lie, even though it seemed to be in everyone's best interest.

After pouring a glass of milk and making a sandwich, Jo sat down at the kitchen counter and started to think about all the things this discovery might explain.

What mysteries have involved water disappearing? Certainly, the question of what happened to water on Mars came to mind right away.

What about Earth?

Have there been bodies of water changed to sand like this in past history? How would we know? With her mind lingering on these questions, Jo went upstairs to get cleaned up.

As she began to fill the bathtub, it occurred to her that the ripples on waves look very much like the ripples formed across wind-blown sand. Could areas that were once seas have been changed to desert in a matter of moments?

Geologists have long taught how rock weathered by wind and waves, breaks down to become the sand of today's beaches and deserts.

This all makes perfect sense and in fact has been proven to be correct.

If it could only be shared, the Starsweep discovery would rewrite history. It could lead to new explanations for the cause of rapid extinctions, fossilization of plants, and animals, and possibly even the origin of life itself.

Could this explain some of the mysteries in the Bible, too?

Jo had always been fascinated by the story of Lot, Abraham's nephew, whose wife turned into a pillar of salt when she looked back as they fled Sodom. Even with a strong faith, her education led her to believe this was not scientifically possible. Now she knows something exists that could explain such a thing, and she can't share it with anyone.

How frustrating!

As she got ready for bed, Jo kept running what they saw in the lab over and over in her mind.

There seemed to be so many new possibilities, but they kept getting overshadowed by the prospect of global extinction.

Jo knew that no one thing on Earth is as critical to life as water. If water disappears, life as we know it will end. It's that simple.

Even the air we breathe is tied to our need for water. Plants produce oxygen, and if they died for lack of water, our breathable air supply would dwindle.

Would Earth then become like Mars or Venus? Were those planets once like Earth? If liquid water becomes sand, what about frozen water?

Mars appears to show evidence of water ice. If the ice melts and comes in contact with this material, it would continue to fall victim to the same fate as water on the rest of the planet. Over time, the landscape would become more and more like a desert.

Climbing into bed, Jo turned out her light and thought about this for hours.

Suddenly she opened her eyes and rolled over to see the bedside clock read 10:00 A.M.

After a quick breakfast, she logged onto her computer to check e-mail.

There were several congratulation messages from friends on the recovery of Starsweep.

There were also two separate, encrypted messages. One was sent by Rick, and one by Jason, with time stamps from last night. Jo knew these would be about their discovery, so she opened them right away.

Reading Rick's message first, it simply stated, "The possibilities seem endless Jo. Let's compare notes tomorrow afternoon." She closed the message and stored it in a secure file.

Jason's e-mail read, "If we look at the bright side of a phase change like this, how many things could be improved by getting rid of liquid water?

Water changing to silica sand might be the key to whole new generations of cheaper and faster computer chips. It could lead to new ways of preventing corrosion, or to stop flooding! We can brain-storm more tomorrow."

Jo smiled and stored Jason's message with Rick's. It made her think about how something this devastating could be looked at from both positive and negative viewpoints.

Jason is looking at the bright side of this, and he is right. There could be a lot of neat things that might be invented or improved based on this discovery.

Jo hated the fact that doom kept overshadowing all the good possibilities.

She decided to drive to the lab and make sure things were secure before their meeting with Ted.

As the security gate opened at the entrance of the lab parking lot, she noticed two trucks parked at the loading dock.

The usual security guard wasn't at the front desk, and when Jo approached the lab office door an armed guard stepped in front of her and said, "I'm sorry ma'am, this is a restricted area. Only authorized personnel are allowed inside."

"There must be some mistake. I'm Doctor Kendesh, the team leader of the Starsweep project. I'm authorized."

"Sorry ma'am. We have orders not to let anyone in without authorization from General Baxter."

In an annoyed tone Jo replied, "Who the hell is General Baxter?"

Suddenly, the office door opened and out walked Ted Preston. "Good morning Jo. You're early."

"What's going on Ted? I know we're supposed to meet after lunch, but I thought I'd check on things first."

"Let's go to my office and talk Jo." Ted raised one arm in the direction of his office up the hall. Jo quietly followed his lead.

Ted opened the door and stepped aside so Jo could enter first. He closed the door behind him and said, "Please, have a seat."

He walked behind his desk and pulled the chair out to sit down.

"Jo, the Security Council met in an emergency meeting first thing this morning. As we speak, the Starsweep and its sample material are being moved to a secret, secure location."

"Are we being taken off the project?" Jo asked.

"No. The three of you are the most knowledgeable people we have on this subject, and we can't afford to lose your expertise.

We do need to put the project under wraps though, so each of you will be screened for our highest security clearance."

Jo nodded and said, "What will the public and the science community be told is going on? They certainly will be waiting for updates on our discoveries."

"The public will be told the Starsweep took on seawater during recovery and the samples were contaminated. Some of the Apollo mission moon dust is being prepared in just this way, and it will be used as a kind of decoy."

"Ted, does the Security Council really think salty moon dust will fool other comet specialists?"

"They hope so Jo. Since no one has ever seen comet dust before, it might be hard for them to say what they're looking at isn't real."

"Come on Ted, you and I both know the age of the material won't be right. Objects like the Johnson-Taylor Comet are from deep space. They're leftovers from the birth of our solar system. It's ancient by comparison to the moon."

Jo added, "I doubt it will take too long before someone matches the decoy to moon samples like a fingerprint.

They'll know something's up and start asking questions."

"It's the best plan we've got so far Jo. Any other ideas?"

"Jason is one of the world's leading authorities on comets, so he might have some idea of how to come up with fake comet dust."

"We need to move fast Jo. The media's expecting regular updates, and once we publish an analysis the other labs around the world will be anxious to get their hands on some of the material."

"If you don't mind Ted, let's skip the meeting after lunch. How soon and where will we get access to the Starsweep material again?"

"Your security clearances are being arranged now. The military will handle your transportation to and from the secret lab site. You won't know where you're being taken, and everyone's access will be limited. There will be other government scientists studying the material properties as well. This will allow us to learn as much as possible about this stuff in the shortest period of time."

Jo responded, "I understand."

"Thanks Jo. I know how much this project means to your team, but it's a whole new ball game now. Who knows what could happen if any of this gets into the wrong hands."

With that, Jo stood up and headed for the door.

She turned back and lamented, "You know, I never dreamt we'd be trying to make fake comet dust as part of this project."

He replied, "I guess there's truth in saying reality is stranger than fiction. Oh, by the way, you don't have to worry about a budget on this project any more either. I've been assured we'll be given everything we need to study and protect our findings."

"No budget? I keep thinking this is all a bad dream, and I'll wake up soon."

Ted poured a glass of water from a pitcher on a side table, took a drink and said, "You know, I've never been a very religious person Jo, but in the past twelve hours I've been thinking a lot about how many simple things we take for granted."

While staring into the glass as if it were a crystal ball Ted asked, "Have you ever seen someone die of thirst?"

"No, thank God I haven't," she replied.

"Someday ask me about time I spent in a prisoner of war camp." He looked away from the glass with a pained expression, and a chill ran up Jo's spine.

She spoke up to break the tension, "Like I said I'll get back to you right after I've met with Rick and Jason."

"Thanks Jo, I'll be waiting to hear from you."

As Jo was leaving the building she saw Rick coming across the parking lot, and Jason was just pulling in. Waving, she motioned for them to join her.

"Hi Jo. It looks like we all wanted to get here a little early."

"Hey Rick. I just talked with Ted Preston, and the Security Council has made some decisions on how to handle this."

Jason approached them and said, "Hey guys, are we ready for the meeting?"

Jo replied, "I just met with the director, and he filled me in on what's happening. Let's go grab something cold to drink, and I'll tell you about it."

They each climbed into Jo's car and she drove for a nearby outdoor cafe. The place was a small ma and pa operation that would be safe for them to talk without worrying about the risk of being overheard.

At a round table on the edge of a brick-paved eating area, they took their seats. Large umbrellas covered each of the tables, which were scattered among ornamental shade trees. There weren't too many other customers, and the table they picked didn't seem to be within hearing distance of anyone else.

Their drink orders were placed, and after being served, Jo began with, "It's probably no surprise we've lost control of our comet project. The Starsweep, the samples, and all the lab equipment are being moved to a secret location, so even we won't know where it is."

Rick proclaimed, "This stinks! Are we being taken off the project all together?"

"No. The government realizes we're the best authorities they have on this, so we will still be helping with the research."

"Helping?" Jason asked.

"There will be other scientists working with the material to speed the research," she explained.

"We will be taken to and from the new lab location in secrecy. There's too much at stake for this to be handled any other way. New security clearances are going to be issued to each of us, and the bottom line is our comet research has become top secret."

Rick asked, "So who's in charge? The FBI? The CIA? The NSA?"

Jo responded, "I didn't ask, and Ted didn't say. To me, the worst part of all this is being convinced our discovery would rewrite a great deal of history, and we can't share it with anyone."

"Not to mention all the good things it might be used for, that now can't be considered," Jason added.

Rick retorted, "Always the optimist. I swear Jason, if we knew the sun was going to flare and burn the earth to a crisp, you'd be the first one standing outside with a marshmallow or a hot dog on a stick to make the best of it."

Jason gave Rick a dirty look, and Jo spoke up before it got ugly. "Cut it out! Nobody planned for this to happen, but it has, and now we have to deal with it.

Jason's right. There could be so many good uses for this it's unbelievable, but the fact is, it could also be the end of us all. Cooler heads have decided it's best to side with caution rather than risk our whole planet turning into a desert, followed by some government official saying, 'OOPS!'"

Jason mumbled, "This would be great material for the Sunday comics!"

Jo took a sip of lemonade and said to Jason, "We have a special task for you my friend. You're our expert in comet geology, so we need to create what amounts to fake comet dust to share with the rest of the scientific community.

The government story is going to be that the Starsweep took on seawater during the recovery, and the sample material was contaminated. They thought using moon dust might fool them, but I reminded Ted the age of the dust wouldn't be right.

Can you come up with something convincing?"

Jason responded, "You're kidding, right?"

"I wish I were, Jason. I wish all of this was a big joke, but it's not. You're a creative guy, can you do it?"

Sitting back and thinking for a bit he shared, "Maybe the moon dust angle would work. You're right that it wouldn't be old enough to match traditional theories about comet age and origins, but this comet is anything but normal.

We could report a theory that when the moon's material was blasted away from the earth, what became this comet was simply a chunk shot off into space during the impact. Like a pool ball that shattered and flew apart."

Rick nodded and said, "That might work. Other astronomers can see that this comet is more rock than ice.

I'm not sure how anything else could be faked to be the proper age without looking suspicious. Just for effect, let's have them throw a trace of diamond dust in with the moon dust and sea salt. That would give the public something to get excited about when they think of comets."

Jo said, "I like it guys. Ted told me there's no budget tied to this project anymore, so adding a little glamour might add to the distraction we need."

Jason jumped in with, "The heat and pressure from an interstellar impact that big could certainly turn carbon into diamond, so why not?"

"Now I'm curious," Jo said in a quiet tone of voice. "Do you guys know anything about Ted's background, or anything about time he spent in a P.O.W. camp?"

Rick responded, "I read a report saying he was a Navy Seal during the Vietnam War. Apparently, he was involved in a mission that didn't go as planned and part of his group got captured.

He and one other prisoner were released after negotiations just before the U.S. pulled out of the war. There were three other guys with them that weren't that lucky though. Why do you ask, Jo?"

"Well, at the end of our discussion this morning he kind of creeped me out. He asked if I had ever seen someone die of thirst."

Shaking his head Jason said, "What a horrible way to go. I can't imagine what it would be like for someone to die like that.

It blows me away that something as abundant as water is here on Earth, could suddenly be so threatened.

Think about how tough those divers are that we watched risk their lives to keep the Starsweep from sinking. It's hard to believe our simple need for water could become the end of us all."

Rick added, "And now we may know why there aren't any other water covered planets or moons in our solar system unless the water's frozen."

Noticing the time, and to lighten the mood, Jo changed the subject and summed up their meeting with, "We need to go. I'll let Ted know what we've discussed, and find out what our lab access schedule will be. I'll also get our transport details and get back to you.

They finished their drinks and rode together back to the Starsweep lab.

Pulling into the parking lot, Jo noticed the two trucks that were at the loading dock earlier were gone now. When they went inside, they found the lab to be empty, and all traces of the Starsweep had vanished.

Jo turned to Rick and Jason, and commented, "Welcome to the top secret world of comet study."

They soon found the government didn't waste any time getting word out to the media that the comet material was contaminated during recovery.

An official news release had been given to the TV networks and the print media, and Jo knew she still had to deal with Susan McCalum at IBC.

She drove straight home to give Susan a call, and continue planting the seeds of a media cover up.

Susan picked up her direct line right away.

"Hello, this is Susan."

"Hi Susan, this is Jo Kendesh with NASA calling."

"Jo! I'm so glad you called. What's all this we're hearing on the wire service? It says your space ship sprung a leak and took on seawater?"

"Unfortunately, it looks like that's what has happened Susan. We're not sure yet how this might affect what we find in the chemistry of the comet dust, but it will make the job of sifting through the data harder, and it will take longer."

Susan asked, "Can I use that as a quote Jo?"

"Sure. I'll try to keep you posted on what we're finding as time goes on."

"Thanks Jo, I appreciate any news you can share. Maybe you can call before this stuff ends up on the wire service next time. When everyone is reporting the same thing it can come across as being a little boring. Remember our conversation?"

"I understand Susan. I'll see what I can do to throw you a scoop or two if you can keep promoting our research."

"Now you're getting my drift, Jo. Thanks again, and I'll be waiting to hear from you."

As Jo hung up, she wondered if Susan distrusted her.

There can be a feeling that everyone is being told only what the government wants them to hear when the wire service is their only source of information.

If Jo were to feed Susan an exclusive about their comet material containing something like diamond dust, she may be able to use the media to their advantage in future promotion for research funding. Even though she has been told this project doesn't have a budget to worry about any more, there were always future projects to think about.

Back at her apartment, Jo sent a secure e-mail to Ted Preston, outlining what she discussed with Rick and Jason. She also shared her thoughts on leaking a diamond dust story as an exclusive news item to a source in the media that tends to promote their research. If Ted agreed with this strategy, they may be able to get more benefit from it than anyone thought possible.

At the same time, Jo kept thinking about what a tangled web they would be weaving if lies and deception became standard practice.

She thought about how ironic it was that the dust collection took place on Ash Wednesday, which serves as a humbling reminder that we will all eventually return to dust.

This whole situation drove home the point that no matter how advanced mankind thinks it's getting, nature is still in charge.

Jo laid down on her couch to catch a quick nap, and before she knew it, she found herself caught up in a strange dream...

A playful, faithful dog was being sent to fetch a far thrown stick in a grassy field. After waiting for what feels like an eternity, it returned waging its tail.

As she approached the dog to take the stick, she realized it had a live hand grenade in its mouth.

The dog dropped the grenade at Jo's feet and sat wagging its tail, in anticipation of another toss.

Jo immediately woke up in a cold sweat and decided it was time to find out how soon they would get access to the comet material again.

There was so much to be learned, and there was no better time to learn it than now.

Before she could pick up her smartphone to dial Ted Preston's number, it began to ring.

"Hello?"

"Hi Jo, it's Mom. How are you doing today?"

"Good Mom, how are you?"

"Fine dear. We just read in the paper that your space probe had a leak? Will this hurt your research?"

"Well, we're not sure."

At this point Jo became uncomfortable, because now she found herself needing to lie to the woman who brought her up and taught her right from wrong.

"I really can't talk about it much right now Mom, but I'll let you know what I can as soon as possible."

"Okay Jo. Your father says hi, and be sure to take care of yourself."

"I will Mom, thanks for calling. Goodbye, I love you guys!"

As Jo hung up, she wondered how many times over the years her parents kept information from her, or told little white lies to make things go more smoothly.

She knew there was no way she could have said, "Well Mom, it turns out the probe brought back some stuff that could turn all the water on Earth to sand. If that happens, we're all dead. Have a nice day."

At the same time, she had always felt she could tell her parents anything. This is the first time she could recall having to keep something from them for their own good.

Keeping a secret this big was going to be harder than anything she's ever had to do.

Jo thumbed through the stack of mail that had piled up during her time at sea and noticed an advertisement from a business selling solutions for leaky basement problems.

There were also ads from places selling water softeners, water filters, swimming pools, sprinklers, and car washes. They seem to go on and on.

She thought about how our lives are so centered on water that we don't even realize it.

Laundry, dishes, gardening, cooking, cleaning, there isn't a thing we do that is not somehow affected directly or indirectly by our need for water.

If the world's population knew there was something in nature that threatened the water supply like this, what would happen? Jo tried not to think about it.

She refilled the automatic feeder on her fish tank, and thought about the devastation that would occur if oceans, lakes, and rivers were to become nothing but desert wastelands.

It was becoming more and more evident how critical it would be for Jo's team to find out how far this reaction could go. If this was truly a chain reaction, a small amount of material could destroy vast quantities of water.

There would be far less to panic about if the reaction was found to have limits, and could only change finite volumes of water.

Jo realized it would still only be a matter of time before someone might try to use it as a way to terrorize others and gain power.

This whole situation could easily turn out to have bigger consequences than global nuclear war. It would cause vast amounts of destruction and terrible loss of life in a very short period of time. People caught in such a scenario might be the lucky ones. If the world's water supply suddenly disappeared, most of life on Earth would end in slow agony and terrible fighting.

There is no place to hide from needing water, and it would become scarcer by the day. No shelter will quench a thirst. No weapon could be used to make things better, but people would undoubtedly use them to try and control whatever water might still exist.

It would seem that for anything to survive, it would have to migrate to where water remained frozen. Having to melt ice to obtain water would become a new way of life.

Not enough plant life would survive to support the world's oxygen needs. In cold climates, the growing season would be too short. Not enough grain would grow to meet the food needs of the world's population.

The resulting struggle for survival could easily cause wars over who would control the dwindling resources.

Whoever might control the distribution of water on Earth would also control where and how life would continue to exist.

How could nature play such a cruel joke on itself? A sudden lack of the most abundant liquid on the planet could be what erases life from existence.

The more she thought about it, Jo wasn't sure she could bear all of this without sharing it with someone, someone close, whom she could trust with the biggest secret in the world.

As she continued to consider the situation, she realized it wouldn't be fair to put such a huge burden on any of her friends either, so it would have to stay within the close circle of NASA associates she has been working with. Rick and Jason have become about as close as anyone she's known throughout her life, so they would have to be her sounding board for whatever might take place through all this.

Besides, the highest national security clearances are not issued to just anyone. Folks are not supposed to tell their trusted friends, "Now be sure not to tell anyone our secret." Tremendous panic would occur if everyone told their friends. In this case, the panic could certainly lead to a catastrophic loss of life around the world.

Just as Jo was ready to shut down her computer, she noticed the symbol indicating an e-mail message had just arrived.

It was a securely coded message from Ted, telling Jo the Security Council had accepted their suggestions.

Preparations were being made for a mixture of moon dust, seawater, and a sprinkling of appropriately-aged diamond dust to be released to others in the scientific community.

The e-mail gave Jo the go ahead to speak with her contact in the media about the sample contamination issues, their moon breakaway theory, and the traces of diamond material.

Last but certainly not least, the message outlined where and when Jo's team was to meet for continued study of the comet dust.

Jo acknowledged her receipt of the message and shut the computer down.

It was time to call Susan McCalum, then fill Rick and Jason in on what was to happen next.

Chapter 5

Top Secret

Jo dialed the IBC number she had for Susan and after two rings heard, "Hello, this is Susan."

"Hi Susan, it's Jo Kendesh with NASA. How are you today?"

"Great, Jo! How are you?"

"I'm fine thanks. I have an update for you on our comet sample research, and I thought I'd pass it along before the news wires pick it up."

"Oh thanks Jo! I'm sure we can work together for everyone's benefit. What have you got?"

"First Susan, I'd like us to agree that when information is passed on like this, ahead of an official release, that you indicate it came from an undisclosed source."

"Not a problem Jo, standard procedure. If we used your name as our source you'd have everyone calling you for the same kind of advanced information."

"That's right. If we have an agreement then I'll go on."

"Agreed. Let me grab a note pad. Okay, what is the latest?"

"Well, as you've heard, the Starsweep took on water during the recovery mission. The added saltwater means our work will be slowed down. Trying to determine what's from space, and what's from Earth, will take more time than it normally would have.

There has also been an unexpected find in our early work, though."

"Oh really? What's that?"

"Trace amounts of diamond are in the sample."

"Diamond? You mean like in jewelry?"

"It's not gem quality by any means, but it may tell us a lot about how this comet formed.

Our sample material is amazingly similar to the moon dust the astronauts of the Apollo missions brought back."

"Were there diamonds in the Apollo dust, Jo?"

"No, but keep in mind we only got moon samples from a few small areas.

This whole thing leads us to believe this object we're calling a comet may actually be what amounts to a chunk that spun off in the early days of our Earth's formation.

Theory today suggests our moon formed after a massive collision broke a huge chunk away from the Earth.

This comet may be a large, leftover piece from that impact."

"So where did the diamonds come from?"

"The tremendous heat and pressure from an impact that size could easily have caused the diamond formation.

Diamonds are formed when carbon is pressed hot enough and long enough to crystallize."

"Wow, this is amazing, Jo! So the Johnson-Taylor Comet may actually be remnants from a collision that created our moon?"

"That's the way it looks right now, Susan.

As we continue our studies, we'll be sharing some of the Starsweep samples with other scientists around the world. Their review will help us verify and further develop our theories."

"Jo, this is exciting! It's exactly the kind of thing I was talking about when I said we want to work with you on breaking news. Can I set up a formal interview with you to go over this after it's been officially released?"

Jo replied, "Sure, Susan. Any interest we can spur with the public will be a good thing. Just let me know when and where you'd like to talk, and we'll set it up."

In a hurried and excited voice she said, "This is great, Jo! Thanks so much for this information. I'll get right on it, and our next news brief will have a feature on the latest news from your Starsweep probe mission."

"Thanks Susan, I'll look forward to our meeting. Goodbye."

As Jo hung up, she had mixed emotions about how well the conversation went. It not only sounded good, but her media friend ate it up.

Word of diamond material being found in the comet dust should spark interest and the imaginations of people around the world. It might also trigger a frenzy for riches like the old gold rush days, if there were a way for others to reach the comet. Since it took years of planning to get to this point, the odds of others getting their hands on more of this material would be very slim. With the comet heading back into deep space, it would be tough for others to question the story too.

At the same time, Jo felt uneasy knowing there was danger in even having this material around. Who knew what could happen from the knowledge they gained while studying it?

After receiving a text message from Ted, Jo called Rick and Jason to tell them they were to meet in one hour at a local shopping mall entrance.

A van will pick them up for transport to the secret lab where the Starsweep has been moved. Jo was given a description of the vehicle and a code phrase the driver will use to acknowledge the trip.

Rick and Jason were already by one of the mall entrance doors when Jo arrived.

As she approached, Rick said, "Hey Jo, have you heard the latest news brief in the media from your friends at IBC?"

"No, what did they say?"

"Our comet may be a leftover from the collision that formed our moon."

Jo replied, "Imagine that! Did they say anything else?"

"Something about traces of diamond being in the sample, and that they may have formed during the impact."

Jason chimed in, "Where do they get this stuff? Too many sci-fi movies?"

Jo chuckled, "I think it comes from watching too much Star Trek."

Motioning for them to come with her she said, "Follow me."

Rick and Jason followed Jo to one of the mall parking ramp entrances. She looked at her watch and in no more than a minute or two, a green service van pulled up.

The driver's window came down and Jo heard, "Excuse me Ma'am, can you give me directions to something called the Starsweep Lounge?"

Jo responded, "Sure, in fact you can take us there."

The van's side door opened, and the three of them climbed inside. Jason closed the sliding door behind them and took a seat.

This van had a rather plain, but comfortable interior, with no side or rear windows. There was a solid partition between the driver's area and the passenger compartment, so they couldn't see out and no one could see in. Interior lights near the floor created a dim atmosphere, so it took a few minutes for their eyes to adjust.

Rick asked Jo, "Any idea how long this ride will be?"

"None whatsoever," she replied.

"We'll be picked up at different places each time we're taken to the lab."

Jason suggested, "Since there's no budget for this, you'll have to ask Ted for a stretch limo with a snack bar next time. This ugly service truck stuff is pretty boring."

Looking at Jason, then at Jo, Rick said, "I don't suppose traveling like rock stars would fit in with being very secretive now, would it?"

Jo squinted at Rick in the low light and said, "Not unless they put the Starsweep in the basement of a recording studio."

The rest of the ride was pretty quiet. They all understood the need for secrecy, but not knowing where they were headed or how long it will take to get there, wasn't their idea of fun.

After about a 45-minute ride, the van pulled into what felt like a downward facing ramp and came to a stop.

The driver's door could be heard opening and closing, and soon the side door slide open.

The gentleman at the door said, "Please follow me." He turned and walked toward a door where armed guards were posted on each side.

The concrete structure they were in had no windows. The lighting and atmosphere reminded them of the underground bunker facilities at NASA rocket launch sites - very military, very clean, and no nonsense.

Jason shared his opinion by saying, "This place gives me the creeps."

Jo was walking a few steps in front of both Jason and Rick, and was right behind the man leading them to the Starsweep lab. "Given what we're here for, I guess having the creeps might be appropriate."

At the end of a long corridor, they came to another locked door. Their driver placed his chin on a pad and looked into an identification eyepiece. Only an authorized eye print match would open the door.

The door unlocked, and they entered a large room that housed a smaller room. There was an air lock entryway into the small room, which was much like the Starsweep was in at the NASA lab. They could see the Starsweep and all their equipment inside.

Their escort turned to Jo and said, "Your director will arrive shortly. Once you go through the decontamination room and suit up, you're free to carry on your research."

Before Jo could respond to say thanks, the driver turned and left the room.

Wanting to get at their work as soon as possible, they each quickly climbed into their protective suits. Once inside the lab, they set out to find out how far the water conversion reaction will go. They set up a measured, but microscopic amount of the comet dust to react in a similar fashion to what Jason did earlier.

This time their observations would be recorded using high-speed digital equipment, under several different wavelengths of light.

After many hours of experimentation, some of their worst nightmares were being confirmed.

A comet sample the size of a pinhead had turned over 200 gallons of water into sand. There didn't appear to be any end in sight for how far the reaction would go yet, either. The conversion reaction they continued to witness was unlike anything they had ever seen in nature.

Once the liquid water changed to silica, it became as dormant as the sand on a beach. The reaction seemed to take place between the atomic and molecular level, so any water touching itself as one body continued the reaction until all the liquid was converted.

It was a little like watching water freeze in fast motion, except the result was a warm, dry, sand pile.

If water had actually gotten into the sample container in the Pacific, the world's oceans might have changed too quickly to imagine.

Their experiments also showed frozen water is not affected by the comet material. Something about the structure of ice crystals does not allow the reaction to take place. Once the phase change occurred from solid ice to liquid water though, all that was left after the reaction is sand.

Since the reaction also produced some heat, it could cause melting and further reactions around the polar ice caps. This could continue until low arctic temperatures finally offset the reaction heat.

As their work progressed, Jo, Rick, and Jason remained quiet as they tested what would happen to the dense water vapor we know as clouds.

They discovered if this material were to blow in the wind, the clouds could turn from white, billowing cotton balls, to dark, raging dust storms. Rain would turn into sand while falling to the ground. Only frozen hail would make it to the ground before it melted. The ice balls would create crater impressions in the sand. These would be in danger of turning into the same sand as their surroundings when they melted.

The researchers realized their findings began to explain the existence of certain types of craters that don't appear to have a solid core buried at the center.

This could also explain the sudden appearance of huge, global dust storms on Mars.

When Ted arrived at the lab, Jo, Rick and Jason took the opportunity to go over their initial findings, and it was almost too much for the team to grasp.

They asked Ted to help arrange a quick experiment that evening at a military base swimming pool.

The experiment would be done after hours, so the pool would be closed and locked. A microscopic sample from the Starsweep would be placed in the pool, to see how far the reaction could go. They figured no one would suspect anything if the pool was closed for cleaning or maintenance.

Ted made the necessary arrangements for the pool experiment before the team was transported back to the mall entrance. He told Jo she would find a message in her e-mail explaining when and where to meet for the pool test.

When Jo got back home, her smartphone alerted her of a short message that read, "9:00 P.M., Officer's Club, at corner of Crawford and Walker Street. Uncle Sam will bring the water toys." The same e-mail message was copied to Rick and Jason.

Jo made her way to the nine o'clock meeting and discovered the facility was in the middle of being remodeled. She found it to be locked up, and looking like a construction zone, so it would be perfect for their needs. No one should have reason to suspect anything.

Carrying a briefcase, Ted arrived with two other gentlemen who were wearing white, one-piece maintenance uniforms and hardhats. He found his three team members anxiously waiting by the front door.

One of the gentlemen unlocked the door, let everyone in, gave a wave in the direction of a car passing slowly by on the street, and then re-locked the door behind them.

Ted shared, "This place may look like a rather deserted construction zone right now, but I assure you we have several friends keeping this area secure."

There are a number of lights on throughout the building, with plastic sheets covering work areas and various ladders standing around.

The swimming pool in this building was in the lower level. As part of the remodeling, it was scheduled to be removed as a budget cutting measure.

If the sample test were to show what the scientists think it will, they may help speed the project along without anyone being the wiser.

As they entered the pool area, they saw several large hoses being used to speed the filling process. Clear water was now about four inches from the pool deck.

The taller of the two gentlemen that arrived with Ted left the room, and a few moments later the water flow stopped. The other one removed hoses from the pool and threw them off to the side.

He then used a floor squeegee to dry the deck around the pool. The first gentleman returned, and the two of them made sure the deck area was dry up to the edge of the pool. They also checked cable connections on two data collecting computers that had been wired to the pool.

Ted said, "Without going into too much detail, we're not taking any chances here. We want to be sure there are no water paths from the pool to other areas. They're not just turning off the water supply valves, there are also several feet of the connecting pipe to the city water supply and to the drains being removed. This area will be totally isolated from contact with other water sources.

Can you imagine the panic that would take place if suddenly every running water faucet in the city clogged shut and filled sinks, toilets and swimming pools with sand?"

"Good thinking," Jo responded.

Once everything looked in order, Ted said, "Thank you gentlemen, please take your stations outside the room, and we'll call if we need you."

With that, they both left the pool area and closed the door behind them.

Ted opened the briefcase he was carrying. Inside a separate, locked compartment was a small glass capsule about the size of an aspirin tablet. It had a small lead fishing weight attached like an anchor.

He put on protective gloves and a cover suit, and then handed Jo, Rick and Jason cover suits too.

While they put on their protective clothing, Ted set up a wide-angle video camera and an infrared imaging camera on two separate tripods.

As he focused the cameras toward the pool he activated them to record, and explained, "This pool holds 500 thousand gallons of water. This glass capsule has a microscopic sample from your comet inside. The attached weight will cause it to sink when tossed into the water. The glass thickness and shape is made to burst at a water depth of five feet.

When the capsule breaks, the sample will come in contact with the water and we will witness the first large scale test of how far this reaction might go."

He noticed the team was intently looking at the capsule.

"Is everyone ready?"

They looked at each other and nodded yes.

Ted picked up the capsule, and tossed it toward the middle of the pool.

All eyes focused on the small splash the capsule made as it slowly sank near the center.

Being so lightweight, it slowly and gently fluttered downward.

Suddenly, the capsule burst and a faint rumble could be heard as the pool deck began to shudder.

From the center of the pool, a change could be seen taking place that was both mystifying and horrifying.

In a matter of two or three seconds, the clear water in the pool could be seen changing from the center outward, into what looked like a grayish tan solid.

The circular ripples caused by the capsule hitting the water were frozen in place, and soon the change throughout the pool was complete.

A slight hissing sound could be heard which might have been due to the reaction still taking place under the surface material that had already changed to sand.

There was a noticeable rise in room temperature.

A few seconds passed, and Ted picked up a small cup of water he had sitting by one of the camera tripods.

He threw it on top of what once was a pool full of water. When it hit the surface, it merely created a wet spot and appeared to sink into the sand.

The fresh water didn't change when he put it in contact with water that had already been transformed.

It appeared, only water that's in contact with the initial reaction goes through this strange alteration.

How such a small amount of material could transform such large volumes of water is still a mystery, but this showed the scientists what might have happened if water had really gotten into the probe during the recovery at sea.

Jo thought to herself, the result would be unthinkable if someone or something were in the water at the time this occurred.

Jason turned to Ted and exclaimed, "Cool!"

Jo slapped at the back of Jason's head and said, "You're nuts!"

He ducked to dodge her swing and said, "Hey, we just saved these contractors the time and trouble of having to fill this pool with sand. That's incredible!"

Rick finally spoke up, "I still can't believe this reaction just keeps going with such a small amount of material. There has to be some kind of limit to it."

Jo asked, "Does there? Can you stop a supersaturated liquid from turning to a solid once the reaction starts?"

Ted added, "Until now, those changes didn't represent a complete, irreversible change from water to sand! This goes beyond being scary!"

Walking toward the pool, Jason put his foot out onto the sandy surface and gave a little push to check the stability.

The group watching looked at each other with concern, but they understand what Jason was doing.

He found it to be as stable as any sand he's ever walked on, so he applied more weight and moved the other foot out onto the once liquid surface. With both feet on the sand, he carefully took another step, then another, and soon decided it felt safe enough to walk across the entire width of the pool.

Jason turned around, came back toward the others standing by the camera tripod, and said, "This is just amazing. You know, now we'll have to try this on a remote lake somewhere. If there's a limit to the reaction, we have to know what it is.

A limit would mean it could be harnessed as a useful tool, just like this was, just like I've been saying all along."

Jo said, "But Jason, if there's no limit we'd have a bigger problem on our hands than the nuclear meltdown at Chernobyl."

Ted said, "The scientist in me agrees with you Jason, but my gut says no. Doing this to a remote lake would likely destroy all the life in and around it.

What if this capsule had been dumped in the Gulf of Mexico? Could what we just saw happen to the world's oceans?"

Rick added, "Not cool."

Jason responded, "Ted, the pioneers of nuclear physics had no idea if the first atomic test would start a chain reaction and destroy the world. They had a pretty good idea it could be controlled, but they had no guarantees.

This stuff is a part of nature, and it seems to me that we need to understand it if we hope to survive living with it."

Ted looked at the floor, shook his head and replied, "That may be true, but the nuclear threat is lower, because of how difficult and complex it is to manufacture the materials needed for weapons.

This stuff could be mishandled far more easily.

It's great to have discovered another possible cause for the extinction of dinosaurs, but we can't risk it causing the extinction of humanity.

We need to know a lot more about this stuff before larger scale tests take place.

I know this test was necessary, but given the results, I'm almost sorry we did it.

What are your thoughts, Jo?"

"Honestly Ted, my first thought was for the sake of life on Earth this stuff should be destroyed.

I think Jason makes a good point about it being part of nature, and that we need to try and understand it in order to survive with it."

Rick commented, "I agree. No pun intended Ted, but we can't stick our heads in the sand on this."

Jo looked at Rick with a bit of disgust in her expression, but she knew what he meant.

"A larger scale test may be the only way we can truly find out how far this reaction will go with a given amount of the comet sample."

Ted thought in silence for a moment as he gazed at the sand-filled swimming pool.

Then he spoke. "I value your opinions on this, but it scares the hell out of me. I'll take these results and the video back to the Security Council and find out where we go from here.

Let's get out of here and meet again in my office tomorrow morning at eleven o'clock." Ted went to the door and stuck his head out to let the gentlemen he came with know the group was ready to leave.

They picked up the video gear, left the pool deck area and locked the door behind them.

One of the gentlemen pulled a small hand held radio from his cover suit pocket and said, "All units, prepare to secure the area."

As they descended the front steps of the building, Ted said to the group, "By late tomorrow morning we'll have a decision from the Council on what to do."

The next morning, the team waited anxiously in Ted's office for the Council's decision.

Ted entered the room and walked to a relief map of the U.S. hanging on the wall. He spent a few moments looking at the desert mountain ranges of the northwest, turned to the group and said, "Good morning!"

Rick took a sip from a giant carryout cup of coffee and asked, "So, what did the Security Council decide?"

"After the Council reviewed our experiment, watched the video, and discussed the pros and cons of the next step, a decision was made to run a full scale test in a remote, high desert region of Washington State.

An isolated lake will be chosen to run the test, where there should be limited environmental impact.

Of course, we all realize you can't dry up an area where water is already scarce and not change the local eco-system. This means we'll be doing an environmental impact study as well."

Jo added, "In a lot of ways this makes the first nuclear test seem like child's play."

Jason walked to the map and said, "If we find a limit to the reaction in an isolated lake, we'll be getting closer to understanding another mystery of nature."

Meanwhile, as Rick intently scanned the map he said, "It seems to me this is really no different than if a drought dried it up. It happens all the time."

Jo responded, "No one has ever seen it happen so quickly though, at least no one that's been around to record it for history.

If someone asks, how will the government explain an entire lake disappearing?"

Ted moved his hand over a region on the map and explained, "This area has a long history of earthquake and volcanic activity. Ever since Mount Saint Helens erupted, the general public has been aware of how quickly and violently nature can change the landscape. Activity that may drain a lake shouldn't be too hard to explain."

Jo added, "Except that there's usually some kind of big wet spot left where the water was."

Jason commented, "Hey with that in mind, this stuff could be great in super absorbent diapers!"

Everyone looked at Jason with a bit of puzzlement, and Rick once again somehow missed his mouth with his big cup of coffee.

Pointing at the fresh spill, Jason continued, "We could probably use the entire comet sample just following him around!"

Trying not to laugh during such a serious discussion was hard, but everyone knew Jason's sense of humor helped cope with the tension.

With a stern look, Ted crossed his arms and stood with his feet shoulder width apart as he looked at the group.

"Kidding aside folks, in two days we will be in south-central Washington, at the Yakima, U.S. Military Training Reserve. On a nameless lake located between there and the U.S. Department of Energy, Hanford Site, we will observe a top secret, full-scale experiment.

If anyone asks where you'll be for the next few days, tell them you'll be attending an out of town business meeting and you can only be reached through the office.

Now, we have several things to arrange before this test, so later on be sure to check your secure e-mail for travel details.

Dismissed."

This was the first time Jo could recall Ted being so short with her team. The worries of doing this full-scale test in the open environment were beginning to show.

As they left Ted's office, Rick poked Jason in the shoulder and said, "Diaper absorbent."

Jason replied, "Hey, I wasn't kidding! Think of the possibilities!"

"Possibilities? Here's one, the user pees and ends up becoming a sand sculpture!"

Jo interrupted their quibbling with, "Knock it off you guys! You sound like my little nephews!

We need to pack. I'll see you back at the lab after I've run an errand."

Chapter 6

The Race Is On

As Jo drove to a nearby convenience store to pick up some much-needed travel supplies, she turned on the car radio.

She happened to catch a brief news story on the latest Starsweep information.

It covered everything Jo had discussed with reporter Susan McCalum, but there was an alarming addition to the story.

The radio report concluded, "It has also been reported over international news wires that a European Union (E.U.) satellite will also attempt to bring some of this unique comet material back to Earth for further study.

Be sure to stay tuned to your local IBC radio or television affiliate for all the latest breaking news and sports updates."

Suddenly, Jo whipped into the store parking lot, screeched to a halt and yelled, "Oh my God!"

She quickly fumbled through her briefcase to find her cell phone. In frustration, she dumped the contents on the passenger seat, grabbed the phone, and frantically dialed Rick's number at the lab.

After a few rings she heard, "Hello?"

"Rick, it's Jo. You're not going to believe this! I just heard a news report that an E.U. satellite is going to try to bring back some of the comet material too! Good Lord, what are we going to do?"

"Settle down Jo, I'll contact Ted and try to get more details. This isn't good. Maybe your contact at IBC can fill you in a little more?"

Without covering the phone receiver, Rick yelled across the lab to Jason. Jo had to pull the phone away from her ear, because his voice was well above a comfortable volume.

"Jason! Jo's on the line and says she just heard a report that an E.U. satellite is going to bring back more comet material."

Over the phone, Jo could hear banging and crashing in the background.

She heard Rick say, "Are you okay?"

In a softer tone, he speaks into the receiver to Jo and said, "Jason was balancing on the back two legs of his chair, and he fell over when I told him the news."

"Is he all right?" Jo asked.

Rick responded, "He's fine. He'll be on the line with us in just a second."

A click could be heard on Jo's end as another line picked up.

"Hey Jo, Jason here. You're kidding, right?

"I wish I was! We need to get ahold of Ted right away and figure out what to do about this."

Rick said, "If an E.U. craft brings more of this stuff back we're all in for big trouble. I'll try to get with Ted right away. How soon will you get back here?"

"I'm in a store parking lot right now, and I still need to pick up some things for our trip to the lake. I should be back at the office within an hour."

Jason added, "I don't think this news will change the current test plans, but I'm sure it will speed up the urgency for us to learn as much as we can, as fast as we can."

"You've got that right! I have to go. I'll see you guys back at the lab."

As he hung up, Rick told Jo to hurry.

The travel supply list Jo was running through her head before the radio report had disappeared from memory.

She thought to herself, "It's time to concentrate on the here and now. What do I need? Aspirin, toothpaste, deodorant, and maybe a prayer book."

On her way back to the lab, Jo thought about her conversation with Rick and Jason.

She decided calling Susan McCalum at IBC might be a good idea to see if she could get any more details on the news report.

Jo frantically dialed the cell phone with her thumb as she slowed with traffic coming to a stoplight.

"Hello, this is Susan."

"Susan! Hi, this is Jo Kendesh with NASA."

"Hi Jo. Do you have more news about your comet for me?"

"Not right now Susan, but maybe you can fill me in a little more on the report I just heard about someone else bringing more comet material back?"

"Oh, yeah. Doesn't that sound exciting Jo? At least you guys at NASA did it first, right?"

Jo chuckled, "That's right! We brought it back first so we should get top billing. Do you have any more details you can share about our competition? Things like who, how, where and when?"

"As a matter of fact, Jo, I do. When can I set up an interview with you again, so we can get a follow up on your latest discoveries?"

"Well Susan, I'll be out of town on business for a few days, but once I'm back I'll give you a call and we'll set it up."

"Great! I'll be expecting your call."

"So who else is planning to bring some of the comet material back? "

"Our sources tell us the European Union has a satellite returning to Earth that's been on a yearlong mission studying the sun's solar wind.

It turns out the craft has some ability to pick up a limited amount of dust from the comet's tail as it heads away from the sun.

I guess the news of diamond material being part of the comet dust created enough interest for them to try and bring their own material back."

"Gee Susan, given the problems we ran into with getting clean, dry samples back to Earth with a mission specifically intended to do the job, I hope their craft is up to the task."

"Jo, do I sense a bit of protectionism in what you're saying? It almost sounds like you want to keep your comet samples and research as an exclusive study."

"Oh no Susan, not at all! I'm sorry if I came across that way. I never want to downplay anyone's effort to expand our knowledge of the universe.

I was thinking we could probably help them avoid some of the mistakes we made during the recovery if they're interested in learning from our experiences.

Do you know when their craft is scheduled to return?"

"I don't have all the details in front of me, but I think it's in a few weeks. By the time we meet for your interview we should both know more."

"Thanks Susan. I'll call you when I'm back in town."

"Have a good trip Jo. Where did you say you were going again?"

Trying to avoid answering any more questions, Jo crinkled an empty snack wrapper near her cell phone to sound like static and fade in the connection.

"I'm losing our signal Susan. I think my battery's going dead. I'll be in touch again soon." That was too close, Jo thought.

What started out as a ploy for some extra media attention and better public relations, was suddenly becoming more than she cared to deal with.

As she continued the drive back to her NASA office Jo shook her head in disbelief. How has a project that started out to be so straightforward turned into such a threatening situation?

They've already discovered that very small amounts of the comet are dangerous. If others bring more of the same material back, and accidentally expose it to the world's major water resources, it would mean disaster.

After pulling into the lab parking lot, Jo went through the usual security checks then rushed to find Rick and Jason.

Approaching her office, the door flew open and she nearly got run over. Her coworkers come barreling past and in mid stride said, "Follow us. We're heading to Ted's office to go over what's up with the E.U. situation."

Ted's office door was open, and they entered to find another gentleman in the room with him. He motioned for them to have a seat and said, "Please join us, and close the door."

Jo, Rick, and Jason found some empty chairs and prepared to focus on Ted's every word.

Addressing the team, Ted started, "This gentleman is Doctor Morrison, and he's a member of the Security Council. He also works with our government's intelligence agencies. The news of an E.U. satellite attempting to bring more comet material back is obviously a major threat, and he's here to update us on the situation."

Doctor Morrison nodded and said, "We haven't been in contact with the European Space Agency because of what we already know about the material."

Jo interrupted, "But wouldn't you want to get in touch with their highest ranking officials to warn them about our findings?"

The doctor replied, "Absolutely not. I know you all have the highest security clearance on this project, but I'll still make a stern warning that what I'm about to say is not to leave this room.

We are not comfortable with sharing what we've discovered, because we don't believe the European's security is tight enough to keep the information from getting into the wrong hands."

Rick asked, "So how will we keep them from bringing material back to Earth that could wipe us all out?"

Morrison responded, "Unfortunately, this is where things get ugly. All I can say is that the E.U. satellite will never make it back to Earth."

"What?" Jo exclaimed. "How can you stop it?"

The gentleman from the council replied, "In a few days, as the European satellite gets closer to Earth it will experience an unfortunate malfunction."

While staring at the ceiling, in a matter-of-fact tone of voice, Rick stated, "So their craft will be destroyed before it gets back to Earth?"

He then turned to look at Morrison.

Nodding his head yes the doctor said, "In a nutshell that's what has to happen."

Jason asked, "So will their solar wind project information be lost too?"

"Not really," Morrison replied.

"Their satellite has been transmitting most of the data it has collected over the past year. It wasn't until after the Starsweep brought back samples that the Europeans decided to try their own off-the-wall collection and recovery operation."

"Won't their satellite burn up during re-entry if it wasn't meant to come back in the first place?" asked Rick.

Ted replied, "A typical satellite would burn up, but since theirs was built to study the sun, they feel the heat shielding might be able to pull off a small sample recovery.

We obviously can't sit back and let them attempt a re-entry when we know there's so much at stake."

Jo asked, "Are we sure it can be disabled before it gets too close?"

In a smug tone, Doctor Morrison answered, "Let's just say we're confident the E.U. craft won't be making it back to Earth."

Closing her eyes and rubbing her temples Jo asked, "Are we still going ahead with the lake test?"

Ted answered, "You fly west at 10:00 P.M. tonight. If you haven't seen the travel details yet, Rick and Jason will fill you in."

Ted took a drink from an open bottle of water that'd been sitting on his desk.

He raised it toward the small group and said, "Here's to the most abundant liquid on Earth, and God willing, may it stay that way."

Morrison added, "We'll see you tonight at the airstrip, nine-thirty sharp."

That evening Jo, Rick, and Jason found themselves pulling into the airstrip parking lot together in almost a parade formation.

They pulled luggage from their trunks and walked toward a small, twin-engine jet, beginning to warm up on the runway.

Ted waited by the stairway of the plane and handed each of them a sealed folder labeled with their name. Two security guards took their bags and loaded them into the cargo hold.

Ted leaned toward Jo's ear and shouted over the noise of the engines, "Review these before the test. You should have a smooth flight! The weather is good, and everything is being set up to run the test tomorrow night!"

Jo leaned toward Ted's ear and yelled back, "Why at night?"

He replied, "We don't want any uninvited guests seeing anything strange from above. I'm flying out later, so I'll see you there."

Jo nodded and climbed the stairs behind Rick and Jason. Once inside, an armed guard closed and secured the door.

The jet engines sped up, and the plane pulled away toward the runway. Ted watched as the plane took off and traveled west.

Once the plane had reached cruising altitude, Rick noticed what appear to be lights in the distance that were traveling in the same direction and at about the same speed they were. He leaned over to look out the window on Jason's side of the plane and saw similar lights on that side as well.

He commented, "It appears we have fighter escorts tonight."

Jo had already opened her folder and was reading the test brief.

Without looking up from the pages she commented, "With what we're headed for, I'm not surprised. This test is going to be amazing."

Jason was reading his information too, and said, "Where did they get enough of these things to cover an entire lake?"

"What are you talking about?" Rick asked as he opened his information packet.

Without looking up from his reading Jason said, "The entire lake is going to be covered with a blanket of artificial, floating, rocks.

They will create a thermal blanket to hide the expected temperature increase from heat imaging satellite cameras.

In other words, spy satellites won't be able to see a big hot spot when the test takes place."

Jo commented, "Using the hollow, man-made rocks will help make the lake look like the surrounding area if someone is taking spy pictures from above. During the day, to a plane or satellite, the scene will look like typical desert terrain.

They've figured out how to camouflage an entire lake!"

Rick spent a few minutes reading his information to find out what Jason and Jo were talking about.

He became more fascinated with what he was reading and said, "How have they pulled all this together so quickly? I'm glad these guys are on our side."

The rest of the flight was quiet as the three scientists finished reading the information and tried to get some rest before the big test tomorrow night.

In the early morning cloak of darkness, their plane landed on a remote airstrip at the Yakima, Washington Military Training Reserve.

Their luggage was unloaded by military police, and they were driven to a housing complex where they would stay during the test.

As their belongings were taken to their rooms, the officer in charge told the group, "Your director will pick you up in the morning.

Breakfast will be served at 0800 hours, and you will leave for the test site at 0900."

Jo asked, "So that means we leave at 9:00 A.M., right?"

"That's right ma'am," he replied. He then saluted, turned, and left the building, passing two guards posted at the front door.

After a short, restless night there was a knock on Jo's door at 8:00 A.M. sharp. She opened it to find a small, wheeled cart has been left with breakfast, and a selection of beverages.

While getting ready for a long day she consumed some fresh fruit, a blueberry bagel and a glass of orange juice.

She then headed for the front entrance to meet Rick and Jason, and found them nervously waiting near the door.

"Good morning guys, did you sleep well?"

Rick turned and looked up from his cup of coffee saying, "Sleep? What's that?"

In a tired voice Jason said, "Morning, Jo. I laid awake all night trying to imagine what a lake covered with floating, fake rocks will look like."

"Well, in a bit we'll find out. Here comes a van, and it looks like Ted's driving."

One of the guards opened the front and side passenger doors and Ted said, "How was your flight?"

Climbing into the front seat, Jo said, "Not bad. We were fascinated by the information packages, and I don't think Rick spilled a drop of coffee."

Jason chuckled and said, "Ah, but the day is young," while Rick carefully climbed aboard with cup in hand.

A guard closed the van doors, and Ted pulled away. "We have about an hour drive on back roads to get to the test site.

It's a dirty run-off lake, about sixty acres in size, with an average depth of five feet. It has no official name, and it's not unusual for it to dry up in drought years.

The lake is shaped like a horseshoe, and it curves around a hill you will see to the east.

Nothing much grows around it, and there's no native aquatic life in it, since the ground has a very high mineral content.

This all means it won't draw too much attention if it disappears, making it perfect for the test."

The road they were traveling on soon turned to dirt, sand and rock. It got rougher by the mile, and after about 20 minutes the group heard "Damn it," from the back seat.

Jo and Ted look at each other and without looking back Jo stated, "That would be the coffee."

Jason could be heard commenting, "Nice mess," followed by laughter and, "I can't take you anywhere."

The area around the test site was a high desert. Scrub brush, beige sand and rocks were about the only things to be seen. As they got closer, they noticed a desert camouflage tent was set up near a rocky flat.

"So where's the lake?" Jason asked.

"You're looking at it," Ted replied. "The floating rocks used to hide the rise in temperature are already in place. They are random sizes and shapes, and blend in perfectly with the surrounding landscape. It's hard to tell where the lake starts and stops, because everything is pretty much the same color. What looks like a field of rocks in front of us, is actually our test lake.

Jason's eyes squinted toward the rock field as he marveled, "Amazing! Can we take a closer look?"

The van came to a stop in a cloud of dust, and the team got out. The temperature outside was about 95 degrees, and the humidity was very low.

Ted picked up a softball size rock, and threw it in the direction where he said the lake was. A splash could be heard, and wave motion could be seen as ripples moved along the shore.

The lake's dirty, beige water, covered with floating rock-shaped objects, blended in so well with the ground color that it was hard to tell where the shoreline started.

Rick mumbled, "This is incredible."

They headed back to the van, and Ted drove to the tent. Inside there was a crew setting up banks of computers and camera equipment that would be used to record and study the test data.

Ted explained, "Much like our swimming pool test, a small sample of the comet material will be released into the lake, and we'll study everything we can about the reaction. We're comfortable that this body of water isn't connected to any ground water sources, so the reaction should be limited to the lake area.

We've added one more twist to the test. It raises some ethical questions, but it covers an area that can't be ignored.

We're going to find out what happens to plants, fish and animals that might be unfortunate enough to be in contact with the water as it turns to sand.

Around the bend, on the far side of the lake, an area has been set up to expose examples of these living things to the test water. A team of biologists and veterinarians will be studying the results."

Folding her arms, Jo looked at the ground and said, "This is scary."

Jason asked, "When will the test take place?"

"11:00 P.M. tonight," was Ted's reply. "There's too much at risk to be doing this again, so we're trying to learn as much as possible from this one large-scale test.

Our own spy satellites are keeping an eye on this area to determine what foreign interests will see if they're watching too.

The test sample will be delivered from a secure site on the base this evening. The lake will be exposed to the material in a similar manner to the swimming pool test.

Three dimensional computer modeling has been done on the lake so we know how much water is here. Sensors have been placed throughout the lake, so if a reaction limit is reached we'll know how much water was consumed. The data will be processed with a preliminary report being ready by sunrise."

On the drive back to their base quarters, Ted told the team he would pick them up at nine o'clock tonight.

"Try to get some rest this afternoon," he said. "It's going to be a long night."

Chapter 7

Doomed

Standing in front of the lodge, Jo's watch read 9:00 P.M., and the team waited anxiously for Ted to arrive for the ride back into the desert hills.

Headlights turned toward the facility, and the familiar shape of a van drew closer. It pulled up to the building, and a guard opened the doors for Jo, Rick, and Jason to enter. After they climbed aboard, he closed the doors, stepped back and saluted.

Ted turned toward Jo, reached up to adjust the rear view mirror and said, "Let's go learn something."

As they pulled away from the curb, Jo opened her window. Looking toward the last glimmer of sunset, then up at the stars Jo wondered aloud, "How much of an audience do you suppose we'll have tonight?"

Leaning forward toward the windshield, Ted looked up and said, "On a clear night like this it's hard to say."

Rick asked, "Do our people have any idea when or where spy satellites are overhead?"

"Actually, that's why 11:00 P.M. was picked tonight. The spies in the sky we know about should be off angle for a poor view of the lake area.

It was a nice hot day today, so the surrounding ground temperature and the lake temperature will both be up. Ideally, we want them to appear to be the same, so we can hide what takes place."

"How hot do you think an area that big will get from the reaction?" Rick asked.

"Since we've never seen this happen on such a large scale, we don't know. When the reaction takes off, we hope the lake temperature doesn't increase too much above the surrounding ground temperature. The floating thermal cover will help hide the temperature rise, but spies watching with thermal imaging equipment will no doubt wonder why the lake area warmed up so quickly.

When the sun rises in the morning, we hope the view from the sky still looks pretty much like it did during the day.

The only difference we expect to see will be a big dry spot where a big wet one used to be."

Jason commented, "And if only part of the lake changes, we'll know a limit for the reaction. It will also give us a better idea about how to deal with all this."

"Ted, if we find a reaction limit do you think it will change the way we need to deal with the European satellite?" Jo asked.

"I don't think so," he replied. "There's too much at stake for this to become public knowledge. No matter how this test turns out, we're still dealing with the most devastating material on Earth.

Without water, life on our planet is doomed."

With those words, the rest of the drive to the test site was like riding in the lead car of a funeral procession.

Everyone in the van quietly stared out their window into the desert darkness, knowing they're part of a small group who discovered something too terrible for the world to know about.

About five miles short of the lake area, Ted slowed the van to a stop and turned off the headlights.

He told the team they would find night vision goggles under each of their seats.

They needed to wear these, because no regular lights would be allowed past this point.

At night, lights in the desert can be seen for miles, and they did not want to draw attention to the test site.

They each put on goggles and their view was changed to a scene of ghostly images, all the way to the horizon.

Jo was surprised how bright and clear everything seemed even though it was dark outside. At the same time, she thought it seemed a little spooky, because everything looked like the negative image of a black and white photograph.

Ted told the group, "Now you're seeing the thermal image of our surroundings. Looking at the glow of a light bulb with these on would be blinding. Once you get used to them, you'll be amazed how well you can see and get around in the dark desert."

He left the headlights off, put the van in drive and continued driving slowly toward the lake.

As they approached the test area they could see technicians moving about, and they all appeared to be wearing the same kind of night vision equipment.

The water in the lake appeared to be a slightly darker shade of gray than the surrounding shoreline, since it was cooler than the ground.

Jason commented, "This is so neat. It's easier to tell where the water is with these on in the dark than with our normal vision in bright sunlight during the day."

Ted said, "Let's go to the tent to make sure everything is ready for the test."

Once they were inside he said, "In about a half-hour we'll get a call from the Biology Research Group on the other side of the lake. When everything is ready, there will be a countdown just like a launch.

This time the comet sample will be exposed at the water's edge, and the progress of the reaction will be monitored as it moves across the lake.

If you'll excuse me, I need to talk with the commander to be sure everything is on schedule. I'll be back in a few minutes," Ted finished.

While he was away, Jo, Rick, and Jason began to hear a strange, muffled whistling sound in the distance, so they stepped outside the tent to investigate.

Soon they discovered if it were not for the night vision goggles, they would not be able to see what was causing the noise.

Jason pointed across the lake toward an area near the top of the horseshoe curve and said, "Check it out!"

The faint image of an odd-looking aircraft could be seen as it slowly descended toward the ground. As it came to a rest, the sound stopped.

Rick muttered, "What do you suppose it is? It's not a helicopter or a plane."

Jason said, "It kind of looks like the cigarette boats I've seen ocean racing on TV, only smaller. From this distance it's hard to judge size."

Jo added, "If there are people in it, there can't be more than one or two."

Jo tipped her goggles down to try and see if a better glimpse could be had with the naked eye.

With only the stars shining overhead, it was too dark to see clearly, so she pulled her goggles back into position.

Jason asked, "Any clue what it is, Jo?"

"My guess would be the comet sample just arrived in some kind of secret military aircraft," Jo answered.

She then heard a voice from behind say, "Good guess." Ted walked up beside the group and looking at his watch said, "We just got a call from the biology group saying they're ready.

In about five minutes a system check would be run, and if everything looks good the countdown will begin." From across the lake the muffled whistle can be heard again, as the craft rose slowly into the air.

Once it rose a short distance above the ground, the sound seemed to stop. The image drifted quietly toward the northwest, and then suddenly darted away into the night sky.

Ted's wristwatch began to beep, and he walked back toward the tent saying, "Shall we?"

A large wall section of the tent facing the lake had been folded open, so everyone inside could observe the test.

A faint voice could be heard over an intercom saying, "T-minus twenty seconds and counting to reaction time. All systems are a go."

A short pause is followed by, "Ten, nine, eight, seven, six, five, four, three, two, one...go."

The desert air was dead calm, and all eyes were fixed on the area across the lake where the strange craft took off.

Like a wave radiating from a pebble dropped at water's edge, their night vision goggles revealed a brightening due to a temperature increase, beginning to move rapidly toward them from across the lake.

What could only be described as the sound of rolling thunder grew louder and louder with the approaching shock wave.

The voice on the intercom speaker can be faintly heard saying, "The test is under way."

Suddenly a warm breeze picked up from the direction of the approaching reaction, and the tent walls began to flap. The breeze soon became a blast of hot wind blowing dust, debris, and paper throughout the tent.

The ground started to shudder, and a chill ran down Jo's spine, as she watched the shock front pick up speed toward the shoreline in front of them.

Jo grabbed Rick's arm and fought the urge to turn and run. Jason and several others started to take cover behind whatever objects they could find.

In a few brief moments everyone at the test site came to know sheer terror.

The ground trembled, as thunder from the reaction continued to build and head straight for them.

Watching the reaction move faster and faster toward them, Jo finally panicked and ripped off her goggles to face the fast approaching menace with her own eyes.

Others continuing to watch with goggles on seem to be paralyzed, like deer caught in the headlights.

With her goggles removed, Jo still heard the oncoming roar, but could only faintly make out where the change was taking place.

Under the starlight, a slight wave motion could be seen moving at the surface level, in front of the reaction. Behind the leading edge of the reaction there was no movement at all.

When it finally reached the shore nearest them, which was just yards away from the tent, everyone wearing goggles began to scream, shout, turn away, duck, or pull their goggles off as Jo did.

Taking off the goggles ended her ability to see the advancing temperature difference, and it made the whole event seem far less frightening.

Suddenly the wind, noise, and shaking all faded away as quickly as they had approached.

The reaction could still be seen and heard moving around the horseshoe bend toward the Biological Research Group.

Jo could only imagine the horror of being in the water if this were coming at you.

As the rumbling from the other side of the lake faded in the distance, an eerie calm returned to the desert night.

The same hissing sound the team heard after the swimming pool test could be heard coming from the direction of the lake.

"Do we know what causes that noise?" Ted asks.

Rick replied, "We'll learn more from the test data, but it could be from moisture that's not in direct contact with the reaction.

Moisture in the surrounding ground and air might be raised in temperature enough to hiss like a tea kettle."

Ted paused for a moment, and put his right hand to his ear as he listened to an update through an earpiece attached to his night vision goggles.

He shook his head in apparent despair then motioned for Jo, Rick and Jason to follow him as he left the tent. Briskly walking a short distance away from the test area, he turned and stopped.

With folded arms, he looked down and kicked the sand at his feet.

In a solemn tone he shared, "Our fears have been confirmed. First reports say the reaction has consumed the entire lake."

"What happened at the biological test site?" Jo asked.

"We'll know more tomorrow, but it didn't sound good. One comment described specimens looking like they were freeze dried, or had rapidly crystallized."

Suddenly, a commotion of some kind can be heard in the distance, along with a lot of urgent sounding chatter over the radio.

"Now what?" Ted moaned as he broke into a jog back toward the tent.

As the team followed, Ted stopped in his tracks and held his earpiece again. "There's a problem by the biological researchers."

Fearing the worst Jo said, "Oh God, what happened?"

After a moment, Ted went on, "Apparently someone left a drain hose running from a water truck into the lake."

"So?" she asked.

Ted raised and dropped his arms while saying, "Now someone gets to explain how an expensive water truck that was leased to NASA ended up being filled with sand!"

Amused by Ted's frantic gestures, and probably as a release of nervous tension, Jo, Rick, and Jason began to burst out in laughter.

Less than amused Ted said, "Okay, if you guys think it's so funny, you can explain it."

Jo and the others tried to stop laughing for a moment, then burst out again.

Pretty soon, Ted started to chuckle and finally laughed out loud with the group saying, "Let's come up with a story on the way back to base.

In the morning we'll come back and start to analyze what the hell happened here tonight."

During the ride back to the base the team wasn't having much luck coming up with a believable story about how a water truck ended up being filled with sand.

After a lot of discussion, Ted finally asked Jason, "So you really think the company we leased the water truck from will be okay with, "Shit happens?"

Laughing, Jason replied, "If this project doesn't have a budget anymore, we should just tell the outfit that NASA has decided to buy the truck and not return it. It shouldn't be much different than if it were wrecked in a traffic accident, and NASA or an insurance company needed to pay for a replacement."

"Works for me," Jo stated bluntly.

"I guess it wouldn't be the first time our government paid to hide something, but what will we do with it?" Ted asked.

Jason suggested, "Let's think about the positive side of this stuff. We could sink the truck in a small lake, and use more comet material to bury it, instantly. It would be like digging a hole and filling it in without ever lifting a shovel."

"Very funny, Taylor. You should be a standup comedian," Ted mused. "Weren't you there tonight? We get the point that this stuff could have some incredible uses. Unfortunately, the risk of drying up the world's water supply has to outweigh any urge to treat this stuff like a toy."

Rick spoke up, "You know, I've been thinking about all this on a larger scale, and this might be far more common throughout the universe than we'd like to admit. Think about it.

Over years of study and searching, the occurrence of liquid water seems to be a rarer find in our universe than anti-matter.

Life as we know it depends on water, and maybe we're not finding much water elsewhere in space, because this intergalactic sponge material keeps mopping it up."

Jo shared, "You might be right Rick, and that's what scares the hell out of me."

Jo continued, "Should a newly solved mystery of nature be hidden from the public the way rulers kept knowledge from the masses during the dark ages?

Did explorers honestly think the Earth was flat? If they really thought they'd fall off the edge of the world, they probably wouldn't have gone exploring!

Fortunately, until now, there's never been a time in history when something was discovered that could end all life as we know it.

Even the threat of man-made nuclear destruction gives us a measure of control with our own destiny. Do we blast ourselves out of existence or not? Thankfully, so far, for the most part we've chosen not to.

This discovery has started a whole new era, and like it or not, some high level decisions have to be made for what's best to preserve life."

Jason observed, "So you're saying we're suddenly responsible for the preservation of all life on Earth, by trying to hide something we discovered in nature? That sucks!"

Jo replied, "Tell me about it!"

Ted finally interrupted, "Wait a minute! There are people much further up the power ladder than we are, struggling with the same issues. Let's not get too caught up in what we can't control.

Our job is to understand what we've discovered and pass the information on to the decision-makers. Others will have to decide if this is safe to share with the world."

Being caught up in the discussion made it easy to lose track of time, and before they knew it, Ted pulled the van up to the lodge entrance at the base. A guard opened the doors to let the team out.

Ted told the group, "Get some rest and be ready to head back at 8:30 in the morning."

"Thanks Ted, we'll see you tomorrow," Jo said as she closed the door and waved.

Rick and Jason climbed out, closed their side door and waved as well.

As the comet team members bid each other good night and trudged to their rooms, they wondered if it would ever be possible to get a good night's sleep again.

The next morning, after a near sleepless night, the team members climbed back into Ted's green van.

Jo noticed that Jason appeared to be wearing the same clothes he wore during the test.

"Did you sleep in those clothes?" Jo asked.

"Sleep in them? No. For your information I didn't sleep at all last night," he responded.

Ted turned down the van radio and said to Jo, "Did you hear that?"

"Hear what?" she asked. "That Jason didn't sleep last night?"

"No, the news station out of Yakima just reported they've been receiving calls from residents between Mattawa and the Priest Rapids Dam area, wondering what shook the ground and sounded like thunder last night."

Rick quipped, "You'd think anyone living near a military reserve would get used to strange things happening after a while wouldn't you?"

Ted continued, "The report speculated it might have been a minor earthquake, or the result of military anti-terrorist training operations. They said they would try to follow up with more information later today. Our people will probably put more spin on the earthquake story to avoid unwanted attention."

"Any more word Ted, on the biology test results?" Jo wondered.

"We'll visit the command tent site first, and then check out the biology site. I'm half-afraid of what we'll find out happened during those tests."

Ted turned the radio back on to catch the weather forecast for the day.

After some commercial messages they heard, "Today's forecast for Yakima County and the surrounding area is for a high of 94, with winds from the west-southwest, gusting to 20 miles per hour.

Later this morning and into early afternoon, there will be a 70% chance of rain with winds shifting out of the northwest.

There have been flash flood warnings issued for low-lying areas and dry runs, so be on the lookout. This evening rain chances will diminish. Now for the stock market report."

With that, Ted turned the radio off and picked up a two-way radio from a clip on the dash.

He pressed the transmit key and spoke into the microphone, "This is Team One to Camp, do you copy? Team One to Camp, do you copy?"

A few seconds passed, and a response was heard over the radio.

"Team One this is Camp, go ahead."

"Weather reports say there's a chance of some heavy rain in the area today. Do you foresee a problem with that?"

"We've been keeping an eye on the weather too. Everything has been quiet and stable here through the night, but we're not sure what heavy rains may bring."

"Thanks Camp, we should be at your location in about half an hour."

"We copy that Team One, we'll be looking for you."

Ted clipped the hand held radio transmitter back onto the dash.

Rick leaned forward between the front seats toward Ted and Jo, then commented, "It's a good thing we didn't have to deal with rain last night during the test.

If I understand the way this stuff acts, once the reaction has occurred in liquid water it's over.

Any water or rain that might fall on the material after the reaction takes place, simply remains water, unless it comes in contact with more fresh comet material."

"That's what we've observed so far," Jo confirmed.

Jason said, "I have a question. Now that the whole lake area has been filled level with sand, where will run-off that used to flow into the basin go?"

Rick looked at Jason and tilted his head in an odd manner. "Good point! The water sources that filled the lake basin will have to find a new low spot."

The four team members in the van began to pay closer attention to the local terrain. They soon realized that the path they were driving on to the lake was a flood-carved gully that now led up to a flat, rather desolate plain.

What once was a low spot where the lake existed is now higher ground compared to the surrounding desert. When heavy rain brings water rushing from the foothills toward the lake area, it will have no choice but to continue on and form a river right where they were driving.

Because of the terrain, there wasn't a good alternative to this route either. All the vehicles and equipment that were at the lake site would have to come down this path.

Ted told the group, "As soon as we get to the test site we're ordering everyone to pack up and get out. The last thing we need out here now are problems with flash flooding.

I can see how several miles of the trail we've been driving on could turn into a raging river, since there's no more low spot for the water to collect!"

Ted sped the van up, and soon everyone aboard could tell the government didn't intend it to be used for desert racing.

Rick shouted, "Good thing I'm done with my morning coffee," as everyone held tight and tried to keep from bouncing out of their seat.

In the distance, dark rain clouds could be seen looming on the horizon. From the direction of the approaching van, the crew at the test site could see a growing cloud of dust rising as it approached.

One guard at the command tent pointed in the direction of the dust cloud, nudged another guard, and said, "What's that?"

The other responded, "Looks like somebody's in a big hurry."

The van slid to a stop near the tent, Ted jumped out and dashed inside.

With an urgent tone, Ted approached the commanding officer and stated, "Good morning. With heavy rains approaching, we need to pack everything up, and clear the area as soon as possible."

The officer asked, "What's the problem Doctor Preston?"

He responded, "Without any more lake basin to catch runoff from these foothills, the access route will become a river. What's worse, we may not have time enough to get vital equipment out of harm's way. Can we air lift the computer equipment out?"

He had no sooner finished asking his question, than the commander was dialing a red field phone.

"Code Red! Charlie! Bravo! We need immediate chopper support to remove vital computer equipment from the test area." The commander listened briefly for a reply, and hears, "Ten-four! The evacuation team will be there in 15 minutes. Over and out!"

The commander hung up the phone, turned toward the group of technicians in the tent and shouted, "Gentlemen, we have ten minutes to secure all vital computer equipment and get it out to the airlift pad! Let's make it happen!"

Immediately the men began to close and lock shielded computer covers, disconnect cables, and rush components out of the tent.

Ted was amazed how quickly everyone responded to the urgency of the situation.

"Thank you, Commander. We can't run the risk of losing any of this test data in what could become a flash flood situation."

Stepping outside the tent, he found Jo, Rick, and Jason helping the technicians load equipment onto a flatbed trailer behind a Jeep.

After about five minutes of frantic but deliberate activity, the Jeep pulled away. It traveled toward the area where the odd aircraft landed last night before the test started.

While the helicopter transport could be heard approaching in the distance, the commander came out of the tent and informed Ted it would be picking up the vital biological site materials as well.

He commented, "This is a wise move. Reports have just come in from remote range sites that say heavy rains are causing flash floods."

As the helicopter touched down, it blew huge clouds of sand and dust into the air and across the dry lakebed toward the tent. It churned up a tornado of blinding debris, while technicians loaded the equipment.

In less than three minutes, the helicopter rose again, and slowly moved over a small hill to land on the other side of the lake. There it collected equipment and specimens from the biological test site.

Again the engines could be heard increasing in speed. Suddenly it came into view once more, as it rose above the desert hills and disappeared into the distance.

No sooner did the sound from the helicopter fade than the sound of thunder could be heard in the distance.

Bolts of streak lightning started flashing toward the ground as the dark clouds moved closer.

Jo, Jason and Rick run for the van, while Ted asked the commander where the best place might be to ride out the storm.

Ted entered the van to find his team members searching for weather reports on the radio. Most of what they could hear was crackling interference caused by the lightning strikes.

Pointing into the distance Ted said, "We're going to drive as far up that ridge as we can. Others will be headed there too, and from the way it looks, we need to go now! Hang on to your hats!"

Ted put the van into drive and steered toward the ridge. With no real road to follow, he wasn't sure which way to go.

"Why didn't the military give us a Hummer for a trip like this?" Rick shouted, as he hung on for dear life.

"They're not as comfortable as a van, and besides, I never thought hard-core four wheeling would be part of the plan!" Ted shouted back.

As they rocked back and forth and moved slowly up the ridge, one by one, large drops of rain began to splat against the windshield.

Soon, the drops increased in number and intensity. Ted turned the wipers on, shifted into low gear, and gave the van more gas to get to high ground more quickly.

The wind began picking up, and the low wiper speed wasn't adequate, so he turned them on high.

The rain started pounding so hard on the van roof, it sounded like they were riding inside a drum.

Mid morning sunlight was almost blocked out by the dark clouds overhead.

Repeated lightning flashes gave a strobe light effect amongst the booming crashes of thunder.

Now forward motion of the van had all but stopped, partly due to low traction on the wet sandy slope, and also because of Ted's inability to see the ground in front of them.

The wipers were pounding back and forth so hard it seemed they might fly off at any minute. Even so, they still weren't keeping up with the torrential rain that blocked their view.

Jason yelled in a panicky voice, "Will this thing float?"

Ted was too preoccupied trying to steer and maintain control to answer Jason's question.

They began to feel the van slip backward and a bit sideways, as Ted gave it more gas and tried to steer against the sliding motion.

Jo yelled, "Hang on," and the rain came down harder as the van lurched backward.

Ted fought the wheel while pumping the gas and brake pedals to try and find a balance between traction and slipping back down hill.

Suddenly, the van hit a large rock, and turned violently to the right. Ted lost control and the van rolled onto the passenger side with a horrifying crash.

Jo screamed over the sound of breaking glass, as the van slowly began to spin and slide down the slope.

The sound of metal grinding and bending over the rocks was deafening, with water gushing against the van like a waterfall.

Everything went black.

The next thing Jo realized, she was lying in a hospital bed, and a nurse was checking her blood pressure.

Feeling disoriented with a pounding headache, Jo tried to sit up, and the nurse said, "Please don't try to move Doctor Kendesh. You've got a nasty bump on the head and your right arm is broken."

The vision in her left eye was blurred, and the right side of her face was covered with bandages.

Jo asked, "Where am I?"

"You're in the base hospital," the nurse responded.

Jo tried to sit up again and asked, "Where are the others, and how long have I been here?"

Overcome by dizziness, she slumped back onto the pillow.

"Try to relax. Your friends have a few scrapes and bruises but they'll be fine. The doctor will be in soon to review your condition."

Jo closed her exposed eye, hoping it would help stop the room from spinning.

She soon heard footsteps enter the room and recognized Rick's voice quietly asking, "How is she?"

An unfamiliar voice responded, "She has a concussion, the right cheek-bone has a hairline fracture, and her right arm is broken above the wrist.

She'll be pretty sore for a few weeks but should make a full recovery."

Without opening her eye to acknowledge that she's been listening Jo said, "There's no place like home. Where's Toto?"

Rick asked, "Hey Jo, how are you doing?"

Squinting in discomfort she responded, "Just peachy. How are you guys?"

"Ted and I lucked out with just a few cuts and bruises. Jason needed some stitches in his shoulder, but he's doing okay."

"How long have I been out?" Jo asked.

The doctor replied, "You were brought in yesterday during the storm. It was a good thing others were close by and saw your van in trouble.

Things might not have turned out so well if you had slid any further down the hill."

Jo heard more footsteps enter the room, and she heard Rick's voice say, "How's the shoulder?"

Jason's voice responds, "I'll live. How's Jo doing?"

Lying motionless with her exposed eye still closed, Jo softly spoke, "If you guys can make the room stop spinning I'll be okay."

Then she heard Ted's voice say, "Get some rest Jo. We'll fill you in on what happened when you're feeling better. Then you can help us figure out how to deal with the media. If you're up to it we'll be back tomorrow to go over it."

With an incoherent mumble, Jo faded off saying, "Okay, I'm pretty tired now, and I need to mow the lawn, so see you later."

Leaving the hospital, Jo's co-workers climbed into a new military SUV, and drove back toward the test site.

Ted drove along the edge of what once was a narrow, dry-run leading to the lake area.

The desert storm had turned that same path into a raging river nearly a quarter mile wide.

Almost as quickly as the water rose and pushed everything in its path downstream, it started soaking into the desert sand and evaporating.

A few sizable ponds of water were still scattered along the route, but the evidence of a storm was quickly fading as things dried up. Most evidence that is, with the exception of something harder to hide than a water truck full of sand.

As is always the case, the flash flood had picked up everything in its path and carried it down-stream. This flooding was more severe and moved more material than had ever been seen in this area. In fact, this flooding had moved debris all the way to the Columbia River, which flows from Canada to the Pacific Ocean.

Keeping this project top secret now went far beyond hiding trucks, bruises, broken bones and stitches.

The flood had washed thousands of fake, floating rocks into a river system that flows past several highly populated areas. There were so many of these fake rocks scattered over such a large area that they would be impossible to collect.

Surely, the public will start to ask where these things came from and what they were being used for.

Odd things happening downstream from a military reserve always seem to get more than their share of media attention.

How could this be explained away?

There didn't appear to be any good way to hide this or cover it up.

Ted pulled the SUV to a stop, and the three men climbed out to inspect the terrain.

Jason kicked a fist-size rock at his feet, and it moved a few inches with a thud. He walked a short distance and kicked another, but this one made a rather hollow sound and flew several feet through the air.

He then said, "These things look so real! You can't tell they're not, until you kick one or pick it up."

Rick kicked around the ground until he found three of them and picked them up.

"Tens of thousands of these things floating down the Columbia River are going to be hard to explain."

Rick tossed them into the air and started to juggle with them, saying, "Jo's concussion won't be anything compared to this headache."

Ted finally spoke up and said, "Damn it. Why does this stuff always happen on my watch?

Let's keep moving and check out the test site."

Climbing back into the SUV, the three scientists moved on to see what has happened at the lake.

When they pull up to the area, it was difficult to tell exactly where the lake was. The rain had washed all traces of the shoreline away, and the military removed the observation tents while the crew in the van was being rescued.

Everything around the lake had blended into one rather flat looking plain, and huge gullies were now running in every downhill direction across the desert.

Some of the channels that formed the largest floodwater erosion paths have been scoured down to the bedrock.

Ted wondered, "What do you think would have happened if the flood hit during the reaction?"

With his hands on his hips, looking down into one of the deep ravines, Rick said, "I imagine the wall of flood water would have looked more like a bizarre landslide."

Rubbing his shoulder near the stitches, Jason commented, "And as the flow kept moving, when it reached the Columbia River, the reaction would have continued north into Canada and south toward the Pacific."

Closing his eyes, Ted tilted his head back, took a deep breath and said, "Heaven help us."

Walking back to the SUV, he opened the door and shouted, "Let's drive back, and hope Jo can help us figure out how to deal with the floating rock problem tomorrow. We need to start sifting through the lake test data, too."

Chapter 8

Media Hype

Ted, Rick and Jason visited the base hospital to check on Jo's condition.

They found her sitting up in bed and drinking apple juice while poking at a cup of pudding.

The bandages over her right eye had been removed, and her cheek was very red, with the eye almost swollen shut.

Discomfort didn't seem to be getting her down when she said, "Hi guys, have you been to the test site?"

Rick removed the cover from a small pitcher on Jo's bedside stand, peered inside the pitcher and said, "We just got back."

Jo realized he was searching for something and said, "It's supposed to be coffee, and you're welcome to it. Now tell me what things looked like in the desert today."

After glancing around to make sure no prying eyes were near, Ted pulled one of the man-made rocks from a small duffel bag and set it next to her dinner tray.

"Remember these?" he asked as he looked at Jo over the top of his sunglasses.

"Didn't they cover the lake with these to help make it look like the surroundings?" she responded.

Jason chimed in, "Well, once they covered the lake. Now they're scattered all over!"

"All over?" she puzzled.

"The flood scattered them everywhere. But that's not the worst part," Jason continued.

Ted interrupted, "Unfortunately Jo, now there are a lot of them floating down the Columbia River, and it won't be too long before the public starts asking questions."

"Oh, that's a good one. And who gets to try and explain a bunch of fake rocks floating down the Columbia?" Jo asked.

Ted took off his sunglasses, rested his chin on his chest, and raised his eyes toward Jo saying, "We were hoping you might have some ideas on that one."

Jo tried to sit more upright in bed, groaned, and shared, "It hurts when I laugh, so stop with the jokes.

I'm supposed to do an interview with IBC when I get back, and it will be hard enough trying to explain what happened to my arm and face. Now I need to come up with a story about why there are rocks floating down some river?"

Rick suggested, "Unless they've had someone tailing you, IBC doesn't have a clue where you are on this trip, so they shouldn't have any connection between your injuries and reports of floating rocks in the Columbia."

"Good point Rick," Ted remarked. "Her injuries could have been from a car wreck, falling off a ladder, you name it."

Jo asked Ted, "Not to change the subject, but what's the latest on the European satellite bringing more comet material back?"

He responded, "No word, but I'm sure we'll hear something about it in the news when there's a malfunction.

Others are covering that problem. Our main task is to find out as much as we can, as fast as we can about the comet material," Ted responded.

"When do you think they'll let you out of here?" Rick wondered.

The moment he finished asking Jo this, a woman's voice from the doorway replied, "If she takes it easy, and can be off her feet for a few days, she can leave this afternoon."

Reaching out to shake Ted's hand she continued, "Hi, I'm Doctor Martin. Beth Martin."

Ted looked at his hand, which was still wet and sandy from handling the foam rock from the duffel, wiped it off on his pants, and shook her hand saying, "Ted Preston."

"*The* Ted Preston? Director of NASA?" she asked excitedly.

"That would be me," Ted replied. "These are your patient's associates, Rick Johnson and Jason Taylor."

"Of comet hunting fame?" she quizzed.

"That would be us," Rick responded in a somewhat tentative tone.

"I'm a bit of an amateur astronomer myself, and I love following the discoveries NASA makes. In fact, I have an astronomy magazine in my office with a feature article on you guys. Would you mind autographing it for me?"

Rick replied, "Thanks for your interest Doc. On the way out, we'd be happy to. Is Jo going to be all right if she leaves here today?"

After examining Jo's chart the doctor looked up and said, "As long as you don't overdo it, you should be okay. I've prescribed some pain medication, but it will make you drowsy, so you shouldn't drive while you're on the meds."

Jo raised the cast on her right arm and said, "Driving with this would be tough anyway. When does it come off?"

"The cast will come off in six weeks. Your records will be sent to your regular doctor, so follow up visits can take place back home.

If you promise to lay low, you can leave today."

As she finished her comments, the doctor noticed the rock on Jo's hospital tray. With a look of curiosity on her face, she reached over to pick it up, saying, "What's this?"

Just as she was about to grab it, Rick snatched it from her reach and said, "Sorry we messed up her tray Doc. She collects rocks, and we thought she might like to see a rare one we found in the desert."

With a somewhat startled and puzzled look on her face she replied, "No problem. I just don't often see people bring rocks to patients as gifts.

I'll have a nursing assistant help Jo get ready to leave, and we'll bring her to the lobby in a few minutes."

Ted said, "Thank you Doctor, it was a pleasure meeting you. We'll sign your magazine on the way back to the lobby."

As they headed for the door, Ted waved and said, "See you in the lobby Jo."

A short time later, an elevator door opened in a nearly empty lobby of the hospital. Ted and Jason watched as Jo was brought out in a wheelchair.

Ted suggested, "Let's find a quiet office and go over our preliminary test data. While we were waiting I got a call with a Security Council update, so we'll go over that as well."

Jason took over for the aide pushing Jo and said, "Thanks, we'll take her from here."

As they moved through a set of automatic doors, Jo saw Rick pull up to the entrance in a new government van.

She turned to Ted and said, "First we fill a water truck with sand, and then we wreck a van. We have to stop being so hard on the equipment."

As Ted and Jason helped Jo into the van, Ted commented, "Equipment can be replaced. Good people are harder to come by, and after this incident, I'm more worried about keeping you guys in one piece than about the status of a van or a water truck.

Let's drive over to base headquarters, Rick. We'll find a place where we can make Jo comfortable and discuss the lake test."

During the short drive across base, Ted turned on the van radio and flipped through the channels. He stopped on a public radio station that was playing a soft, classical melody, thinking some quiet music would help Jo feel more at ease.

At the end of the selection an announcer said, "It's the top of the hour, and time for the latest global and local news.

This morning a commercial airliner from France was forced to make an emergency landing in Oslo, Norway, after one of the engines failed. No injuries were reported and a complete investigation is under way to determine the cause of the problem.

In another piece of breaking news, the European Space Agency has reported losing contact with their Solar Wind probe on its return journey to Earth."

Everyone in the van looked at each other and leaned closer toward the radio as they listened intently.

Rick turned up the volume while the radio report continued, "Officials say if they can't regain contact with the probe, hopes of bringing back more material from the Johnson–Taylor Comet could be lost.

Interest in bringing more material back to Earth has grown, since original samples studied by NASA revealed it could be debris left over from the formation of the moon.

In state and local news, fishermen on the Columbia River near Richland, have reported picking up large numbers of what look like floating rocks. Reports say they appear to be man-made, and are similar to what Hollywood might use on a movie set.

Officials don't seem to know where they came from, or what they may have been used for, but they're quick to add they don't expect them to have any harmful impact on the environment.

Next up, the market report."

Ted turned off the radio and said, "Well, I knew it wouldn't be long before this hit the news, but it spread faster than I thought it might."

In a soft, but audible voice, Jo said, "The media already planted the seed that these things look like something Hollywood uses. Maybe we can build on that story and come up with a believable accident that sent a load of fake rocks down the river. Do we have more of them in a warehouse somewhere?"

"I'll check," Ted replied. "If so, we should be able to make it look like they got away from a film crew north of Richland. If not, we'll have more made so we can create the story. Hollywood isn't the only place that can fake reality. In fact, I'd say Hollywood could learn a thing or two from the military and the government."

Ted pulled the van up to the front of base headquarters and shared, "I have arranged for an office area to be set up for the team's use during Jo's recovery. The security desk personnel will show you where it is."

Jo insisted, "I don't want anyone fawning over me, while I'm recuperating. I appreciate everyone's concern, but we need to stay focused on figuring out how to deal with the comet material. I'll get in touch with my broadcasting contact to try and simmer down the floating rock story, too. At the same time we need to keep Rick and Jason working on learning more about the comet material."

Rick and Jason nodded as Ted responded, "I couldn't agree more. You guys keep me posted on your progress, and I'll find out the latest from the Security Council."

They climbed out of the van, and Ted drove Jo back to her quarters so she could get some more rest.

Once inside the new office building, a security guard took Rick and Jason to an office area that looked like a small command center. A large, flat screen, video communication system was on one wall. Three desks with state-of-the-art computer equipment were arranged in a semi-circle in front of the screen so everyone involved in a conference was in plain view. Another wall was equipped with a computerized whiteboard that would allow them to electronically share brainstorming sessions with others.

While the two of them get acquainted with their new surroundings, a guard entered the room and informed them that Jo was supposed to contact her mother as soon as possible. Rick sent Jo a text message that she needed to contact her parents ASAP. Jo texted back, "Thx, will do!"

Realizing it has been some time since she'd been in touch with her folks, Jo picked up the phone and dialed their number. The line was busy, so she decided to see if she could get through on Facebook.

She wrote, "Hi Mom, did you call? Sorry I haven't been in touch for a while, but I've been very busy, and I've also been involved in a bit of an accident." No sooner had her message been sent, than a reply appeared on her screen.

"An accident? What happened, are you okay?"

Jo replied, "I'm okay. Just some bruises and a cracked wrist, so my left hand is typing a bit slow. Can I call you?"

Her mother responded, "Since my old computer is slow and we still use a dial-up connection, I'm logging off. Call me." With that, Jo picked up her cell phone and activated the auto-dial number for her parents. The line rang once, and her mother answered, "Jo, is that you? What happened?"

"Hi Mom. I guess you could say I was in a traffic accident. No one else was hurt, but the van I was in got pretty messed up. How are you and Dad doing?"

"We're fine dear. We hadn't heard from you in a while, and we were beginning to get worried. The news said the Europeans were going to try to bring more of the comet material back too, but they lost contact with their probe. Isn't that a little strange?"

"This is a strange business Mom. When it comes to space exploration, we never know what we're going to run into."

"Well, I don't want to keep you dear. You take care, and keep in touch. If you're still healing from an accident you should get some rest. When will you be coming home again?"

"I'm not sure right now Mom, but I'll let you know. Give my love to Dad, and I'll call again soon."

"Thanks Jo. We love you. Bye for now."

Then she hung up.

The next few days of studying the lake test results were long, and difficult. They also had not produced any real breakthroughs that helped them understand how or why the reaction was taking place. However, the extent of what they learned did seem to prove that the reaction may have no bounds.

With this unsettling knowledge, they went back to Huston and continued their research.

After the team had returned to Texas, Jo decided to try and contact Susan McCalum at IBC. As long as Susan kept getting comet research updates, Jo hoped media hype and speculation could be kept to a minimum. Jo found the number for IBC in her cell's phone address book and activated the connection. To Jo's surprise, after only one ring Susan answered. "Hello this is IBC, Susan McCalum speaking."

"Hi Susan, this is Jo Kendesh with NASA. How are you?"

"Jo! It's good to hear from you, how've you been?"

"Well, I'm a little bruised up and sore from an auto accident, but otherwise I'm doing pretty well."

"Oh, I'm sorry to hear that. I hope your recovery goes quickly. How can I help you?"

"I just called to share that we're becoming more certain about the origins of our comet material."

"Really? That's exciting! I can't wait to hear about it. I suppose you've heard the European Space Agency seems to have lost contact with their craft that was going to bring more comet material back. Any thoughts on what might have gone wrong?"

"I have no idea Susan. Any number of things can happen to a ship traveling through space." In the background, Jo can hear some commotion and papers rustling on Susan's end of the line.

"Just a minute Jo, there's a news update coming over the wire service that might interest you. It's about the European satellite. It says they've been able to re-establish its location and direction of travel. It sounds like they might be able to bring it back to Earth after all. Isn't that exciting?" A long pause came from Jo's end of the line.

"Jo, did you hear me? Are you still there?"

"Yeah Susan, I'm still here. That's great news! Does the report happen to say when they expect it to get back to Earth?"

"The report says that if things work out, the return would be sometime next week. It sounds like they're having some guidance control problems. They're not sure if it will end up being a water or land recovery."

"Susan, can I get back to you? I have a call waiting, and I have a feeling it might be about the European satellite situation."

"Sure Jo, keep me posted on your discoveries, and I hope you mend quickly from the accident."

"Thanks Susan, I'll be back in touch soon."

Jo pushed the call-waiting button, "Hello?"

"Jo, this is Ted. We have another problem. The European Space Agency has just announced they may be able to limp their satellite back to Earth!"

"I know Ted. I just got off the phone with Susan McCalum at IBC and she informed me the European satellite might be back sometime next week. I thought our friends were going to see to it that the European ship wouldn't make it back to Earth!"

"You and me both! The Security Council is meeting in one hour to discuss the situation. Since your team has been at the heart of what we're dealing with, I would like you, Rick, and Jason to be in my office for a teleconference link during the meeting."

"Not a problem Ted, what time would you like us to be available?"

"Eleven o'clock sharp."

"We'll be ready. I'll update Rick and Jason on this, and we'll be there at eleven."

"Thanks Jo, we need your input."

After hanging up, Jo couldn't help but wonder what more could go wrong. She hit her cell phone's speed dial button for Rick's number and listened as it rang.

She soon heard, "Hello?"

"Hey Rick, it's Jo. I just got off the phone with Ted, and he wants us to join him for a conference call with the Security Council at 11:00 A.M. Do you know where Jason is?"

"Yeah, he's still with me at the new office. We've been going over some of the test results, and discussing what could happen if the European satellite makes it back to Earth. We're hoping they find a good way to stop it!"

"We all do," Jo replied. "If it looks like their ship's going to make it back to Earth, they'll need to know what the consequences could be. We were lucky. I don't even want to *think* about what could happen if their satellite makes it back!"

Looking at the clock on the wall, Jo realized they needed to get moving if they were going to make it to Ted's office in time for the conference call.

"Oh man, we need to get moving! Can you guys swing by and pick me up? I can't drive with my arm in this sling."

Rick asked, "Why can't we just patch everyone in by phone, instead of going to Ted's office?"

"Security," Jo replied. "We already have enough problems without risking any of this getting out to the public."

"Okay Jo, we're on our way."

Rick hung up, and Jo slowly sat on the edge of a chair in her apartment living room, anxiously watching out the front window for Rick's car to pull up.

She glanced at some of her vacation pictures hanging on the wall, and thought about how easy it was to take life's everyday activities for granted. They were pictures of good times she has had canoeing with her family, laughing out loud with friends at a water park, and spending a quiet day at the beach to get away from civilization for a while. These are all things people do to relax, but they don't think in terms of how impossible it would be to do them without an abundance of water - an abundance that most of us take for granted.

Just then, Jo heard a horn honk and could see Rick's car pull up. Jumping up, she grabbed her house keys and cell phone from the kitchen table, then dashed out the door.

When she got to the car, she saw Jason riding in the back, and he seemed to be intently writing in a notebook. As she carefully opened the door and slid into the passenger seat, Rick was fumbling with the radio tuner.

Without looking up to see if Jo was having any trouble getting into the car with her arm in a sling, he said, "I've been trying to find news updates during the whole drive over here, and haven't had any luck."

Jo tugs on the seat belt with her good arm and realized the shoulder harness wouldn't fit comfortably over her injury, so she leaned back in the seat and said, "Let's just go!"

Jason continues to write in his book until Jo asked, "What are you working on?"

He replied, "I've been trying to figure out what's going on when this stuff reacts with water. We know that it doesn't react with ice, but as soon as it comes in contact with liquid water a mysterious phase change takes place. Once an initial reaction occurs and more water is added, it only makes the reacted material wet. It doesn't change the freshly added water to sand. Why? It's a one-way reaction that progresses until it consumes every molecule of liquid water that's not separated by some sort of barrier. Nothing more happens unless a new reaction is started with a fresh sample of the material we brought back in Starsweep."

As Rick steered through traffic he said, "This stuff acts like a nuclear reaction, but the atoms don't just split apart the way they do in nuclear fission. They recombine in a new kind of fusion reaction. It's like they're bumper cars, going through fission and fusion at the same time, without exploding or giving off tremendous amounts of heat. Another odd thing is, there doesn't seem to be any special critical mass needed to start or stop the reaction. It doesn't take a certain amount of this stuff to start the reaction with water. Figuring out how and why the change from liquid to solid occurs is one thing, but now we have a life and death problem with trying to keep more of it from getting back to Earth!"

Jo braced herself by putting her good hand on the dash while Rick weaved through traffic. Thinking about everything that has been happening to this point, Jo started to well up, and a tear rolls down her cheek. She put her hand over her face, and with a quiver in her voice she said, "I just hope we can come away from this conference call with a better feeling than I have right now. We started out with a really great project that was supposed to help everyone better understand how our solar system formed. Now we have a top secret mess on our hands that could ruin the planet!"

Jason looked up from his notes and put his hand on Jo's shoulder. This was the first time he or Rick had seen her get so emotional about the situation, and they weren't quite sure how to handle it.

He tried to comfort her with, "Hang in there Jo, we're going to get all of this sorted out. Some day I'm guessing we'll look back at all of this and have a good laugh."

Rick added, "And with all the high level help we're getting right now, I'd say we'll have all this figured out in no-time."

Wiping away a tear, Jo looked over at Rick and responded, "But what I'm afraid of is, 'no-time' is exactly what we have. Trying to keep all the stories straight with everything we've seen in the past few weeks, and trying to deal with the media hype, it's starting to get to me!"

Jason put his notebook down, sat back in his seat, and gazed through the rear side window. He then said, "We're all in this together guys, and we'll get through it somehow. I keep thinking about how ice isn't affected by this stuff, and that alone gives me hope. If the worst should ever happen and our oceans were to become deserts, all the water locked up in the polar ice caps would still be there. It wouldn't be pretty, but life on Earth would adapt. The fact that the only water we've found on places like Mars seems to be frozen, just leads me to believe that poor Mars may have been exposed to this stuff long before life as we know it ever got a chance to take hold."

The three friends remained silent for the rest of the drive, while Jo continued to wipe away an occasional tear.

They arrived at the NASA complex where Ted's office was located and passed through all of the usual security checks.

When they got to Ted's office they found that there were two armed guards standing outside his door checking photo ID's.

A round table was situated in the center of the room, with a speakerphone located in the middle. There were five chairs spaced evenly around the table. As they sat down, they heard footsteps and voices coming toward the entrance. It was Ted and Dr. Morrison, the Security Council member who had assured them earlier that the European satellite wouldn't make it back to Earth.

After the two men entered the room, Ted closed the door behind them. Jo, Rick and Jason stood to greet them. Handshakes were extended to each of them, though with Jo's arm being in a sling there was an awkward moment while Dr. Morrison stated, "The members of the Security Council want to thank you for joining us in this conference call."

Pointing toward Jo's arm sling he continued, "I was sorry to hear about your injury during the storm that rolled through after the lake test. Are you feeling better?"

Jo replied, "Yes, thanks. It should be good as new in a few weeks."

No sooner did everyone sit down, then the phone rang. Ted leaned over and tapped a button to answer, "Hello? Are we connected?"

From the phone on the table, a male voice could be heard asking, "Ted, is everyone present?"

"Yes, we're all here," Ted replied. At this location I'm joined by Dr. Morrison, Jo Kendesh, Jason Taylor, and Rick Johnson."

"Good. On this end we have the other members of the Security Council, who will remain anonymous for security's sake.

We're all here to discuss what must be done to stop the European satellite from landing. We were all involved with the recent lake test, so we understand how imperative it is that more of this material not be unwittingly brought back to Earth's surface.

Dr. Morrison, can you fill us in on what happened and what the next step might be?"

"Certainly," Morrison replied as he leaned in toward the speakerphone. Glancing around the room he continued, "Our attempts to jam or modify the European craft's control signals have failed. We felt it could be made to veer off course to miss the Earth's gravitational pull, but unexpected weather and solar conditions have hampered the effectiveness of our signal jamming equipment."

At that point, an unidentified female voice came from the Security Council's side of the conversation.

"Do you feel the European Space Agency scientists have any idea why their craft has experienced control problems?"

Morrison replied, "No. Since there has been a fair amount of solar storm activity in the past month, the problems they have encountered can easily be attributed to natural interference.

However, our best bet is to make failure look like human error, equipment problems, or some kind of trajectory calculation mistake.

Without question we need to keep it from landing, but we also need to stop short of shooting it down in full view of the public."

The same woman's voice came over the speakerphone again and said, "By the way, we should commend Jo Kendesh for the media piece she did after the Starsweep's landing. At this point there doesn't seem to be anything out of the ordinary with what her study of the comet material is finding. The similarity with moon rock hasn't been questioned by other researchers yet, and the plan to modify moon sample material to fit the story was a stroke of genius. Good work Dr. Kendesh."

Jo's associates look at her as if she should respond, but she just closed her eyes and rubbed her right temple as though she was trying to fight off an oncoming headache.

Ted asked, "If we can't jam their control signal, and we can't blast it out of the sky without causing an international incident, where do we go from here?"

A new voice from the speakerphone replied, "Here's where things get dicey. We can try letting top-level European leaders in on the secret through some less-than-secure channels, hoping we can contain the panic that would occur, or we can go to another level of covert operation to prevent the landing."

Ted asked, "Such as?"

"Ideas have been along the lines of blaming political extremists for directly damaging their ground control facilities, or introducing a virus into their control operations. This would direct the craft back out toward deep space, where it couldn't do any harm."

Morrison added, "We have identified several issues with the extremist ground attack scenario that could make a successful outcome difficult.

I recommend the Council lean toward using a computer virus. Though the 'extremists' of course, would be our own specially trained commandos who could destroy their control facilities, it could still end with their craft crash-landing on Earth.

If we wait too long to take action, even letting the Europeans in on the secret could be too late. They might try blasting it out of the sky themselves, which would only make matters worse by spreading the material over a wider area."

Another voice was heard over the speakerphone asking, "How soon can a computer virus be put in place to stop their craft from making it back to Earth?"

Morrison replied from Ted's office, "As a precaution to try and cover our bases, the code work has already been started for a virus. If the green light can be given at the conclusion of this meeting, our operatives will get new code into the European's navigation system to steer it away from Earth within hours."

Jason asked, "Will this work? Will they be able to steer it away from us? We were told everything would be taken care of before, and it wasn't. What kind of a comfort level should we have now?"

With Jason's questions, everyone in the room looked at him with a bit of an astonished jaw drop. Here was one of their generally quiet technical gurus, asking the hard questions that everyone had in the back of their minds. Everyone else seemed too afraid to ask these things, for fear of what the answers might be.

Looking down at the table, Dr. Morrison shifted uncomfortably in his chair, clasped his hands in front of him on the table, and looked back up at Jason.

With a stern stare directed at Jason he stated, "Mr. Taylor, I wish I could tell everyone here that this is a sure thing. Unfortunately, I cannot. A relatively small number of people on this planet know of the grave danger we're all in. Not just because of the craft that's headed for Earth as we speak, but because of the material that we already possess.

When it comes to matters of our very survival, we have to take action that we believe is in the best interest of everyone. Unfortunately, we don't have the time to discuss these issues with everyone on the planet. This means we have to consult with our best minds and try to come to a consensus. You ask will this work?

During the Apollo 13 crisis, the whole world watched and prayed for the safe return of our three astronauts. They represented all of us, along with mankind's survival in the unknown of space. Here we're faced with the survival of not just three, but over seven billion! All I can add is, in the words of NASA's Mission Control Director at the time of Apollo 13, 'Failure is not an option!'"

A long pause followed before another voice over the speakerphone stated, "I vote we proceed with the virus option. One way or another it could still be blamed on extremists, and if we need to we can still warn the Europeans about what we've discovered."

Morrison interjected, "The problem there would be diplomatic. How do you convince the public that it would be in their best interest to keep them in the dark? Especially when it's something that involves the whole planet's survival?"

Ted looked at his three project scientists and asked, "Any thoughts?"

Jo glanced back and forth at Rick and Jason then took a deep breath before she replied. "If this were all made public, I'm afraid there would be terrible panic based on a never-ending fear that the world could come to a horrible end without any warning. Even though we know a disaster like an asteroid hit could devastate the planet, the threat this new material presents is much greater."

Reaching toward a glass of water on the conference table in front of her, she took a small sip and continued to speak as she set the glass down with a trembling hand.

"This goes against everything I believe about openly shared knowledge when it comes to better understanding the forces of nature, but it seems to me that keeping this a secret is the safest way to go."

With that, Dr. Morrison directed his attention to the speakerphone and asked, "Are the Council members in agreement? Do we proceed with another attempt to stop the European satellite without their knowledge of the situation? If the Security Council members are in agreement with proceeding, please indicate by pressing your pound key."

Over the speakerphone could be heard a chorus of electronic tones that sounded like a dozen or more touch-tone phones having their # button pushed all at once.

Following this, Morrison stated, "If any Security Council member is in disagreement with this motion, please indicate by pressing your star key, and present your case."

There were at least 5 seconds of silence before he concluded, "The vote to proceed is unanimous." He continued, "I want to thank each of the Council members for helping make this critical decision, and you will be contacted if we need to convene on this matter again.

Please keep in mind that any mainstream media reports you hear on the European satellite in days to come, should be taken with a dose of skepticism. Whatever is covered will have been filtered for content prior to release, or their information will be based on conjecture.

Thank you again for your time."

He then poked the disconnect button on the phone, and a dial tone could be heard.

Ted asked Dr. Morrison, "Do you need us for anything else today?"

"No Ted, but I want to thank you and your team for coming. If we need anything more from your group, we'll let you know."

As everyone got up to leave the room, Dr. Morrison put his hand on Jason's arm and said, "Your questions and comments were good ones Mr. Taylor. Our purpose is to keep everyone's safety and best interest in mind."

Jason hesitated for a moment, extended a handshake to Morrison and said, "Doctor, I'm not a particularly religious person, but I'll be praying that this works. Good luck to your people, and let us know if there's anything else we can do to help."

As everyone quietly left the conference room, Jo, Rick and Ted waited in the hall for Jason to join them.

As Jason approached the group Ted said, "With the Security Council's approval that we just witnessed, a virus will be introduced into the E.U. craft's control system within the hour. Those at the top had this plan under development as an option long before this meeting ever took place. This meeting just gave our operatives the 'go-ahead' to make it happen."

"How soon before the European control center will realize there's something wrong with their craft's guidance system?" Jo asked.

"They will know about it before our own equipment can show us how far it might end up off course," he replied.

Ted continued, "My best guess is that by this evening we will see and hear that a new problem with the European comet probe has developed. The real question will be whether the craft can be diverted off course before they discover the problem and correct it. If we don't keep it from entering our atmosphere, I hate to think about what could happen.

You should all go back to the lab and keep trying to figure out how this stuff works. I'll keep you posted on Europe's ship as things unfold."

With that, the Starsweep team departed.

Chapter 9

The Passing

As Jo and her colleagues made their way back to the lab, Jason commented, "We need a way to identify this stuff. Even if it's just a nickname between us, we need to call it something until we give it an official name."

"How about calling it something simple like Fred, or Barney?" Rick suggested.

Jo asked, "Does your cartoon reference from 'The Flintstones' have any significance?"

"Well, the name Barney makes sense if you consider this stuff could turn our planet into Rubble. Get it? Barney Rubble?" Jason quipped.

Jo shook her head and rolled her eyes, while Jason added, "I like it! From now on let's call our comet dust Barney, in honor of Mr. Rubble."

Opening the security door into the lab, Jo said, "Now that we've got that settled, let's see if we can figure out how and why Barney turns water into sand."

Just as they entered the lab, Jo's cell phone rang. She looked at the screen to learn that Susan from IBC is calling. She hit the answer button and cheerfully greeted her with, "Hello Susan! How are you?"

The response was, "Fine Jo, have you heard the latest news about the European satellite that's bringing back more comet dust?"

"No I haven't, what's up?" Jo asked.

"Well, it seems the Europeans have a software glitch that's veering their craft off course. If they can't get it fixed soon the satellite could miss Earth all together. Doesn't it seem odd that they wouldn't have their control program better tested than that, or at least have some kind of backup?"

As Jo sat down at her desk she responded, "Guidance control programs are pretty complex, Susan. I'm sure their best people are trying to get the ship back to Earth in one piece. I guess I would add that everyone should keep in mind that it won't be the end of the world if it's lost. We already have the same comet material from the Starsweep mission, so the European material would be redundant."

"Jo, you almost sound like you don't care if the E.U. craft makes it back or not. Are you getting a little overprotective of your work?"

"Not at all Susan, I just think people should realize the European mission is repetitive of the work we've already done, when it comes to the return of more comet material."

"Okay Jo, you make a good point. Everyone likes a story with drama though, and I'm sure the Europeans want to show the world they can accomplish the same science in space that we can."

"I understand. Will you keep me posted with any more news of their landing progress?"

"Sure Jo, but remember it's in exchange for any breaking news from discoveries with your own experiments."

"Of course, Susan, you will be the first media contact to know when we discover anything new. Thanks for the call and we'll talk again soon."

As Jo hung up, she felt uneasy about the irony of what she had just told Susan, telling her that if the E.U. satellite failed to make it back to Earth, it would not be the end of the world. All along, she knew that if the European craft did make it back, it in fact *could* mean the end of the world. She also thought about what Jason might say to keep things on the lighter side. The last thing the planet Earth needed right now was any more Barney Rubble.

While Jo booted up her computer, she shared what she just learned with Rick and Jason.

"I was just told by Susan McCalum at IBC that the E.U. satellite is in danger of missing Earth re-entry. She mentioned something about a control problem."

Rick looked around his flat screen with a cup of coffee in hand, and said, "Imagine that."

From behind his own monitor, Jason can be heard adding, "It's pretty spooky how fast this all happened. It makes me feel like the meeting we just came from was just a formality."

"At least they bothered to ask our opinion before the plan was put into action," Jo shrugged.

During their exchange, Rick was looking back and forth between his computer monitor and a very large, thick book. After a few minutes of quiet review, he uttered, "Vitric, of having the nature of, or being like glass. It's from the Latin word vitrum, or glass."

"What's that?" Jo queried.

"I'm looking at a more technical name for our mystery material. It causes a never-before-seen phase transformation at the atomic level.

It reminds me of the Hydra of Lerna. In Greek mythology, the Hydra was a seven-headed guardian of the underworld. Every time one of the creature's heads was cut off, two more would grow back. It was one of Hercules' tasks to slay it.

Since some sort of reaction multiplication describes what happens when our comet material reacts with liquid water molecules, I suggest we call the comet material *Hydravitric*.

Hydra is for the expanding beast, and Vitric is the Greek-based word for being glass-like. The comet material makes liquid water molecules turn glass-like on contact, and it multiplies the process until no more liquid is available. It seems that trying to stop this stuff is going to be a Herculean task, too."

Jo responded, "I like it. I will bring it up with Ted, and with his approval we will use the term in our classified reports."

Rick chuckled as he refilled his coffee mug and said, "So tell us, how did Hercules defeat the Hydra? Would his methods be of any help to us?

Just between you and me, I still like the name Barney Rubble, but I suppose we need to use something more appropriate for official use."

Jason replied, "I rather doubt the legend will be of much use. Hercules cut off one head and dipped his sword in its blood, which was the most poisonous venom in the world. He used it to burn the neck stump of each subsequent head he cut off, so it couldn't grow back. One of the Hydra's heads was immortal. The legend says he put the immortal Hydra head under a huge rock along the sacred road between the cities of Lerna and Elaius. He later used the Hydra's poisonous blood on arrow tips to defeat another foe, the Centaur.

Greek mythology buffs would tell you that after Hercules defeated the creature, the gods put the Lernaean Hydra into the night sky as a constellation. This was forever a reminder that Hercules defeated the gate keeper of the underworld."

Rick wondered, "So now, will astrology nuts say that bringing Hydravitric back from space amounts to bringing poisonous blood back from the Hydra constellation? Is this its revenge against Hercules and mankind?"

Jo made a time-out sign with her hands and raised her voice saying, "Let's get a grip guys! Jason's name for this stuff fits, and this is all very interesting, but we have bigger things to worry about instead of how this fits in with Greek mythology!"

With that, Jo's team dove into studying the structure of the material using various instruments that were all protected in glass enclosed isolation cabinets.

Looking at the material with an electron microscope and a spectrometer failed to reveal any clues as to how or why Hydravitric changed water to sand. A definite shift in element signatures was seen, but no clear conclusions could be drawn as to how the transformation was taking place. It was as if some form of cold fusion or cold fission was happening, but without the massive temperature change expected in nuclear reactions that are currently understood by scientists.

They used high-speed digital cameras to study the reaction forward and backward, but had no reference to compare it with. Nothing like this had ever been observed on Earth, unless they applied it to Biblical stories of people turning to pillars of ash during the destruction of Sodom and Gomorrah.

Much like the mysteries surrounding why gravity works, the way this material acted was a complete puzzle. Nothing frustrated Jo's team of highly educated scientists more than seeing something occur before their very eyes that they could only describe as magic.

No scientific reference could be found to describe what they were studying, but other mysteries of the solar system kept crossing their minds. Was this the answer to so many mysteries they still had no explanations for? Mysteries like, why is liquid water only found on the surface of the Earth, and not other parts of our solar system?

NASA and other space agencies from around the world have found overwhelming evidence that there was once a sizeable quantity of liquid water on Mars. The question still remains, where did it all go? Only frozen water exists there now.

Jupiter's moon, Titan, has been found to be covered by an ocean of frozen water. Have places like this throughout the solar system, and perhaps the whole galaxy, been spared from becoming deserts in space, because only liquid water is at risk of being converted to sand by contacting this newly discovered part of nature?

How odd it seemed that so many mysteries about the nature of water's disappearance over geologic history could be explained with yet another mystery. They wondered how big a role this material has played in the existence and evolution of life as we know it.

Without liquid water, life on Earth might not have developed into what exists today. Have other civilizations been doomed by Hydravitric? Have other distant life forms across the universe learned to deal with this part of nature and survive? Have we not detected other life forms on other planets because of it?

All of these questions, and more, kept running through Jo, Rick and Jason's minds, as they feverishly studied the comet dust and wondered how their discoveries might tip the balance of mankind's existence.

Several hours had passed with the team continuing to try to understand the nature of their comet dust, when a security-warning buzzer announced the arrival of someone entering the lab. It was Ted, and he had a concerned expression on his face.

As he entered the room that the team was working in, each of them stopped what they were doing and focused their attention on Ted.

"More bad news just in," Ted announced. We just got word that the European ground team discovered and removed the directional control virus our operatives put into their guidance system."

Shaking his head Rick responded, "Not good."

Ted continued, "The worst part is, they not only discovered the software problem and fixed it, they have the operatives that introduced the virus in custody, and they're interrogating them on why and under whose orders such a thing was taking place. Fortunately, the agents don't know any critical details, other than the E.U. spacecraft was to be directed off course from an Earth landing. They don't know why."

"Do they know the operatives were working for us?" Jo asked.

"At this point we're not sure," Ted replied. "The bigger question is whether they fixed the problem in time to redirect their craft back on course for an Earth landing. Right now, those at the top are deciding if we can take that chance. The Europeans know someone is trying to prevent their spacecraft from returning, and that will make it more important for them to find out why. The Security Council may decide there's no choice but to let certain leaders in Europe know what's been going on. That would certainly need to be kept top secret, and couldn't be allowed to be leaked.

Have you had any luck figuring out more about your Hydravitric?"

Looking surprised at Ted's use of the name Jason came up with, Jo pressed, "How could you know that? We just discussed calling the material Hydravitric this afternoon, and haven't shared it with anyone yet."

Looking down at the floor and then back up, Ted said, "For security reasons and for your own safety, this lab is wired with video and audio surveillance. A select few with top security clearance, including myself, have been monitoring everything that's been going on in this lab while you're working on this project."

With a bit of indignation in his voice, Jason stated, "I guess it's a good thing we didn't say anything we shouldn't have."

Nodding and turning toward Jason, Ted replied, "We all know what's at stake here, and nobody involved should be surprised or offended by the fact that their actions are being watched.

In this case, I have to say the surveillance saved us some time by dispensing with red tape and formalities. We had already been searching for something to call this stuff, and the story you related with the Greek mythology background sounded great. It's descriptive enough for those who know what's going on, and it's cryptic enough for those who don't need to know."

Turning toward Rick, Ted added, "Barney Rubble isn't a bad name either, so if we need a term that's more pedestrian, we can use that one as an unofficial reference. Not in official documents mind you, but just between us, like you suggested."

Rick broke out in a big smile and raised his cup of coffee toward Ted in a salute of approval.

"When I hear more about the E.U. satellite's status I will let you know. In the mean time, Jo if you hear anything more from your media contact at IBC I'm counting on you to keep me posted." With that, Ted left the lab, and the three scientists went quietly back to work.

Jo found herself feeling uneasy with the news that their every move was being monitored at various levels. She wasn't surprised though, given the news that the U.S. operatives in Europe were in custody. They all knew that if the E.U. craft made it back to Earth there would be unthinkable possibilities for a global catastrophe.

What bothered her even more was that only a small handful of people knew what would happen if Hydravitric from the European satellite landed in our oceans.

If more knew about it, would we all be safer, or would we all be worse off, for the panic and uncertainty that it would cause throughout the world?

Jo did not like keeping people in the dark when it came to discoveries in nature. At the same time, she and her team members knew that wide spread knowledge of this could have just as devastating an effect as having the oceans suddenly, and without warning, turn into sand.

She consoled herself with the feeling that some things are better left unsaid. If a natural disaster occurred due to this material, she knew it wouldn't be much different from a world-changing meteorite strike, like those believed to have caused the mass extinction of dinosaurs.

The uncertainties of the immediate situation might be made less dangerous if some of Europe's key leaders knew why their satellite should not be brought back.

Jo hoped members of the shadowy Security Council, and those in charge at NASA would be feeling the same way she was. If they failed to tell the Europeans why they should not bring more of the comet's material back to Earth, it could mean an agonizing end for untold masses of humanity around the world.

Was keeping this a secret a moral thing to do, basing it on a belief that some secrets are too big to share?

At this point, it was beginning to seem to Jo that some secrets are too big *not* to share. With all these issues mulling around in her head, she finally voices her frustration by saying, "Can we really keep this a secret from the Europeans anymore?"

Jason answers, "It wouldn't seem so, but it's not our call. If it had been up to me, I would have told those at the top in Europe right away, rather than trying to keep what we know a secret and ruin their exploration efforts.

On one hand, it seemed like the right thing to do to try to protect others from finding out and risking widespread panic. At this point the leaders probably had no choice but to share what's going on, and they'll look like crooked idiots to the European leaders for trying to do what they thought was the right thing."

Rick interjected, "They would probably have done the same thing. Hopefully they can get past the mistakes that have been made, and get on with trying to save everyone's tail before it's too late."

"Let's hope so," Jo responded.

At that moment, Jo's computer emitted a loud BEEP, alerting her that a high priority message had come in, which required her immediate attention. Jo opened it and read that Ted would be calling in a few minutes on a secure conference call over NASA's computer system. It will involve a video conference between the team and the Security Council members, but the Council member's input will be through voice communication only.

"Heads up guys," Jo announced. "Ted informs me that we will all be in conference with the Security Council in a few minutes again."

"That would explain why my screen has gone blank," Jason stated.

"Same here," added Rick.

Suddenly, all three of their monitors come alive with an image of Ted facing his computer monitor at his office desk.

"I trust everyone can see and hear me," he stated. "Council members have video and audio feeds on this, but for security reasons we only have audio from them."

Jo asked, "What's the latest, Ted?"

"Unfortunately, the Europeans very quickly detected and corrected the software malfunction that was put into their guidance system. Since it's crucial that their satellite not bring more Hydravitric back to Earth, the White House is being informed by Council contacts that those in charge of the European program should be advised immediately that they need to abort their mission."

"Can this be done soon enough to prevent their craft from gaining entry into Earth's atmosphere?" Jo asked.

"Our latest tracking station reports show it will be cutting it very close. Timing is crucial, and our fear is that diplomatic channels may not be able to react fast enough to prevent their ship's return," Ted responded.

Rick asked, "Can't our President talk to theirs, and stop it almost immediately?"

After a pregnant pause in the conversation, a voice from one of the Security Council members interjected, "At this point, our President is still learning about all of this."

Jo got wide-eyed and gasped, "You're kidding, right? The President is just now learning about all this?"

The same voice responded, "In matters of covert, need-to-know secrecy, the President is kept out of the loop to maintain what we refer to as 'Plausible Ignorance'. It keeps top administration officials from being prosecuted by virtue of the fact that they had no direct knowledge of a particular incident."

Jo looked straight into the monitor camera and said, "This is incredible. You're telling us that top officials have been purposefully kept in the dark, so others making key decisions can end up being the fall guy if something goes wrong?"

The voice replied, "Harsh as it may seem Dr. Kendesh, long ago, key officials decided there would be a group of top minds picked from every field to serve on the Security Council. On matters of major importance, the Council would make recommendations and sometimes even crucial decisions in place of our leaders. Especially in matters of grave urgency that do not offer time for debate or that might not be taken well by an uninformed public."

Ted added, "Unfortunately, there is as much potential for harm to be done through world-wide panic as there is from the possible loss of our world's major water resources. The Council was formed to help make decisions that ever-changing political figure-heads are poorly equipped to make."

With concern in his voice, Rick spoke up and said, "So here we are, being the only public faces that represent NASA's work on this comet material, and if it all goes bad, guess who will get the blame."

A new voice from a Security Council member was heard over the computer speakers adding, "Blame isn't the issue right now Mr. Johnson. We can worry about ironing those issues out once we get past stopping the Europeans from accidentally destroying our planet."

Jason responded, "That's easy for someone with no identity to say, but the reality is, we are the only ones with skin in the game right now. The Europeans are just trying to save their space mission."

Jo cut the tense exchange short by asking, "So what's next? How are we stopping the European craft from landing?"

Ted replied, "The President has been briefed, and a call is being made to the Director of the European Space Agency to tell him how Hydravitric reacts with water. The sooner the Europeans know, the sooner it can be stopped."

Jo then asked, "And if it can't be stopped, what is the plan? We have lost a lot of precious time trying to hide what we know, and every minute that passes it gets closer."

"Can it be blasted to bits in space before it reenters our atmosphere?" Jason asked.

Ted explained, "Unfortunately it appears to be too close. Trying to destroy it at this point in space would cause small fragments to rain down everywhere, putting even more ocean surface area in jeopardy. All we can do now is wait and see if they can divert the satellite enough to bounce it off the Earth's atmosphere. If it makes it far enough back for re-entry, I'm afraid all we can do is pray."

A solemn silence filled the room. Had those who thought they had the best interests of humanity in mind, and knew so much, ended up creating their own doom? Only time would tell. Everyone involved knew they were at the mercy of fate more than they were in control of nature.

Ted sensed the awkward silence and abruptly closed the conference by saying, "As soon as we know more about the situation, you will all be notified."

With that, the computer screens on each of the scientist's desks went back to their normal state, and displayed exactly what they were working on before.

Jo and her team were frustrated that mankind has found so many ways to add complexity to its existence. Hiding what they knew seemed as foolish as hiding what they didn't know.

Keeping people ignorant of a dangerous situation was becoming a real moral dilemma for Jo, wondering how and where this might end.

The odds of mass extinctions occurring from an asteroid impact are low, but there seemed to be strong scientific evidence that it has happened before, and it will likely happen again. Do many people lose sleep worrying about an event like that happening during their lifetime?

This was different. Everyone involved with this situation knew that Hydravitric was a real game changer. It neatly and simply explained so many mysteries about why liquid water seems to have just disappeared from planets like Mars. It might answer questions like, where did the water go, and how quickly did the landscape change?

Jo's team has discovered an important piece to some very major puzzles in nature, and now it has gotten caught up in a bizarre web of deception.

On top of all that, if humanity survived the outcome of this mess, it could easily turn into an inquest and blame game that would only lead back to Jo, Rick and Jason.

They realized now that the Security Council members were essentially untraceable, nameless, faceless entities. They also were just told that the President, and others at the top, had been purposely kept out of the loop. That way, the administration could claim ignorance if authorities needed to implicate underlings who could be charged with over-reaching their bounds.

All of this stunk to high heaven, and Jo was becoming more worried about what might happen if the European satellite made it back to Earth.

Were they being set up? Jo was thinking it, but dared not ask Rick or Jason about it for fear they might be wondering the same thing.

She was beginning to wonder where Ted stood on the matter as well. They had always had what she felt was an open and honest working relationship, but his apparent defense of the Security Council acting apart from those in charge really troubled her.

It wasn't clear whether the council worked the way it did, based on orders from the top, or whether somewhere down the line they became a ruling group hidden in the shadows. Were they a group that helped protect the backside of the President's office, while they themselves were protected by the system under a cloak of secrecy?

There was no real way for Jo to know, but her gut instincts told her to be careful. Wanting to be on the safe side, she started to think of ways she could cover her bases without raising suspicions.

After a long day of frustrating meetings and no breakthroughs in understanding the nature of Hydravitric, Jo said goodnight to her colleagues and caught the city bus back to her apartment.

While eating some leftover pizza she turned on the TV to watch the national news. Flipping through the channels she nearly spilled her plate when she found that every station had breaking news reports, or under-screen text streamers, about intrigue surrounding the European satellite landing.

Reports were buzzing with news of someone being held in custody for a covert attempt to keep it from returning to Earth. There were no details on who was behind the attempt. The network anchors all seemed to be interviewing various terrorism experts, who were saying this may be the result of a new level of computer hacking sophistication. Speculation of guilt was pointing toward militant groups who were upset with economic sanctions or military policies of the European Union.

The most disturbing part of the reports came with the prediction that since the effort to ruin guidance control had been discovered and fixed, the satellite was expected to come down somewhere over the south Atlantic Ocean.

With a mouth full of pizza, Jo shouted, "Dear God!" She hit the mute button on the TV remote control, and used her secure cell phone connection to call Ted.

Jo was surprised she had not heard from Rick or Jason if they had already heard the same news reports, but then she realized she had shut her ringer off during the conference calls and forgot to turn it back on again. In fact, there were seven missed calls listed. Three are from Rick, two from Jason, and two from Susan McCalum with the IBC television network.

After two rings, Jo heard Ted answer with a calm, "Hello Jo." His caller ID had obviously flagged him that she was the caller, but it still took her by surprise to hear him answer as though he was expecting a call from her.

"Have you seen the news? Is it true the European satellite is coming down over the south Atlantic?" she urgently asked.

"Unfortunately, it looks like that might be the case," he responded.

Jo followed with another rapid-fire question. "What happened when the President talked with the European leaders?"

With a matter-of-fact tone in his voice he explained, "Well, we may never know what their real reaction was. To say the least, they weren't too happy. The worst part is, by the time they understood the situation it turns out there was no time to steer the craft clear of Earth's gravitational pull. All we can do now is wait and see where it comes down."

"And pray," Jo added.

"And pray," Ted repeated.

"The media still has no clue what could happen from this, do they? She asked.

"No, and everyone at the top wants it to stay that way. Our leaders and the authorities that know about it now in Europe are in agreement. They feel the risk of all-out panic is far too great. There were no calls made or official Council meetings called after all this took place, because there is nothing more anyone can do about it now."

"And how long do we have before it comes down?" she asked.

"Best estimates right now are that it should begin to fall through Earth's atmosphere late tomorrow afternoon.

The European satellite is smaller than the Starsweep was. It no longer has any fuel for maneuvering capability, so it will be at the mercy of nature, while it tumbles through our atmosphere.

If it comes apart during re-entry over the ocean things could get ugly very quickly. If it comes down intact, and the parachutes work like they're supposed to, the weather in the south Atlantic could affect where it finally lands."

"What direction is it coming in from?" Jo asked.

"It will be coming in on a north-to-south, polar trajectory," he replied.

"Ted, is there a chance that it could end up coming down over ice if it travels as far south as Antarctica?"

"That's a possibility Jo, but there's no way of telling with a craft this small and the changing weather patterns around that part of the globe.

This is a long shot, but since you have security clearance I can share that if it looks like the parachutes are going to put it down in rough seas, a chase plane will attempt to snag the chute lines while it's still descending. Then the plan is to carry it to some remote location over the frozen mainland for retrieval.

Everything humanly possible will be done to keep that satellite from landing in the water. We know that blasting it out of the sky wouldn't be safe, so catching it in the air may be our last option."

Jo suddenly heard a knock at her door. Looking through the peephole, she saw Jason anxiously waiting for someone to answer.

"Jason's at the door Ted. Can I call you back?"

"Sure Jo. All we can do now is wait."

Jo hung up, unlocked the door and opened it to find Jason pacing nervously. He nudged his way past her into the apartment and immediately went over to look at the muted TV screen.

"Have you heard what's going on? In the next day or two we could all be toast!"

"I know Jason, but I was just on the phone with Ted, and they have a plan to try and catch the satellite in the air during re-entry and take it to ice-covered land on Antarctica."

"I'm tired of their 'plans' Jo. I'm afraid these idiots are going to kill us all, so I took matters into my own hands."

She asked, "What are you talking about? What have you done?"

"I called your friend at IBC and told her the whole story Jo. If the end of the world is coming, I believe everyone deserves to know before it happens."

"Good Lord, Jason! Do you know what you've done? What if nothing happens? The world-wide panic you may have unleashed could be as devastating as the oceans turning to sand!"

In a hurt tone, he responded, "I tried to call you first Jo, but you didn't answer, so I decided to do something myself."

Suddenly, Jason darted out of the apartment and moments later, the sound of squealing tires could be heard pulling away from the curb out front.

Jo knew she needed to get through to Susan McCalum at IBC and try to put a lid on the potential damage Jason's story could cause.

By violating the secrecy of his security clearance, she knew he not only endangered the lives of countless others, but he put his own life in jeopardy as well.

If credible word got out that a NASA scientist with top security clearance had gone public with what was going on with this project, there would be hell to pay.

Jo immediately called Susan's direct number at IBC but got no answer. She waited for an operator to come on the line and asked if she could be paged, but was told that Susan had left for an important meeting and failed to say when she would return. This worried Jo even more. Was the meeting with Jason? How much information had he actually shared?

Jo knew she had to get in touch with Ted again on this, so she hit his speed dial number and waited as it rang.

"Hello?"

"Ted, this is Jo again. I have some awful news about information Jason may have given to the media!"

"We know Jo, there are agents in the process of finding Mr. Taylor as we speak. As far as his media contact goes, there have been actions taken with the Europeans to make sure nothing is made public that shouldn't be reported."

After Jo heard Ted make that statement a chill ran up her spine. How could the study of something as seemingly simple as comet dust have turned into a manhunt for one of her research team members? And on top of that, how could it have become a life-and-death situation for the whole planet?

Ted tried to settle Jo's nerves by saying, "I know all this has turned into a mess from the beginning Jo, and we all know you're not to blame. We're all in this together, and one way or another we're going to get through it together. We need you to be strong and stay focused on your original mission. Keep trying to figure out the role Hydravitric plays in the universe and everything else should fall into place.

At this point we need to let others worry about how to deal with the information."

Those words didn't make Jo feel much better about the situation with Jason, but they did help bring her part of the mission back into focus.

"Okay Ted, I'll do my best. What's the plan for tomorrow?"

"Let's meet at the lab around nine o'clock in the morning. Try to get some rest, and we'll take things one day at a time."

The line goes dead, and Jo booted up her computer to see if there was any late-breaking news on the Internet.

Chapter 10

Enlightenment

Jo tossed and turned in bed as she thought about what might happen in the next twenty-four hours. She wondered where Jason was, and how Susan at IBC would report whatever information Jason shared with her. At this point, she knew there was not enough time for the media to release news reports that could cause mass panic.

Maybe Jason felt regardless of what happened, he could face the situation with a clear conscience, knowing he tried to warn the world that this was coming. Would it be better if this happened without anyone knowing about it in advance, or would it be better to let everyone prepare his or her own way?

Jo finally came to the realization that if the European satellite broke apart over open water tomorrow, none of these worries would matter.

The sound of the kitchen clock ticking seemed like distant thunder. Try as she might, Jo could not find rest on the eve of what could be the end of civilization.

Did Jason feel he had to do what he could to warn others? Were his actions too little, too late?

Jo was only sure of one thing now, and that was how much of her final destiny would be in the hands of God. She believed trying to control the situation was out of human grasp.

Being a religious person, and believing in The Savior, Jo often thought of the universe and living on Earth in terms of a giant experiment that God was observing. All of the education and best-laid plans of humanity were only one piece in the puzzle of what God may have in store for us.

If all of this came down to a test of free-will and stewardship, how would humanity end up when the final grades are posted? She knew that regardless of our life experiences, we are all destined to die.

Jo knew from her years of scientific studies that energy could not be destroyed, it could only change form. This knowledge helped form a powerful basis for Jo's belief in an after-life. She believed the energy that makes us all unique individuals is not destroyed in death. The energy that defines our soul merely changes form as we move into another dimension.

If it turns out that life is a filter used to sort out the souls destined for heaven, Jo wondered if she would make it through. Will the souls passing into heaven be those that would impose their will on others, because that is what they thought would be best for everyone, or would it be those that were fine with letting others make their own choices?

She knew the final outcome was out of her control. Her faith in a loving, forgiving, God would somehow see mankind through all this. Feeling exhausted, Jo finally rolled over and dozed off.

It seemed Jo had just relaxed with the sweet relief of falling asleep, when a loud and persistent pounding on the apartment door awakened her.

She stumbled to her feet and opened the door to find Rick taking a drink from a large mug of coffee.

"Care for a swig?" he asked, as he offered it in Jo's direction.

Rubbing her eyes and temples, she turned around and took a seat at one of the kitchen counter stools as she said, "What time is it, and what's the latest on Jason?"

"It's about seven o'clock, and I knew you'd want to hear this. Jason called me about an hour ago and said he and Barney Rubble contacted Susan McCalum at IBC. He said he knew no one would believe his story unless they saw what Barney could do with their own eyes. Apparently, he sent Susan a video clip with his smartphone, while he did a little demonstration!"

Rick took another drink from his mug and offered it toward Jo one more time as he said, "You sure?"

Realizing there was probably more in his mug than strong coffee, Jo raised her hand and shook her head saying, "No, but thanks for offering."

Fearing the worst Jo asked, "So do we know where he is now, or what IBC is doing with the video?"

"Couldn't tell ya. Just before he hung up he said he was ditching his phone so they can't track him through the GPS."

"And the video?" Jo asked again.

Rick sat down on the couch and replied, "No sign of the video or Susan on any news that I've heard since his call."

By this time, Jo was wide-awake and in an uncharacteristically excited voice she asked, "So how much Hydravitric do you think he used for his demo?"

Taking another big swig from his mug Rick chuckled, "Hell, knowing Jason he may have used ALL of it!"

"Holy Crap!" Jo exclaimed. "Do you really think so?"

"I'm not sure Jo, but I'm guessing he's wanted dead-or-alive by now. They must have been tracing his calls, because shortly after he hung up I got a call from Ted.

Which reminds me, we were supposed to meet at his office like, five minutes ago."

Jo looked at her cell phone and saw that a missed call from Jason had come in about an hour ago, while she was sleeping. He also left a text message after the missed call.

It read, "I C U B4 U C ME, HYDRA IS DEAD!"

Handing her phone over to show Rick, Jo asked, "What do you make of this?"

After looking at the message for several seconds, he passed it back saying, "Well, I'd say it sounds like he was planning to dispose of it somehow. I hope he hasn't done anything stupid."

Throwing her good hand up and shaking her head in disgust Jo responded, "I'd say he's already crossed that bridge, wouldn't you?"

Suddenly Jo's phone rang. Her caller ID indicated that Ted is on the line, so she pushed the answer button and said, "Hi Ted. What's the latest?"

"Is Rick with you?" he asked.

"Yes, and we're headed your way soon. Is there any word on the satellite, or where Jason is?"

In a strange tone he replied, "We'll discuss all that when you get here."

"We should be there in about 20 minutes. I need a few minutes to get cleaned up and change."

"Okay, Jo. I'll look for you and Rick at about seven thirty."

Hanging up, Jo grabbed some fresh clothes and raced into the bathroom. Rick leaned back into the couch cushions, turned on the TV and took another sip from his mug.

Flipping through the channels as the shower could be heard running in the background, Rick stopped on a station where news headlines were scrolling across the bottom of the screen.

One news item said that evening would mark the expected return of the European satellite. It also indicated the exact splashdown time was still unknown, but early predictions suggested it would be somewhere in the South Atlantic Ocean.

A few news items later, Rick sat up and paid closer attention, as he put his drink down on the coffee table. The streaming headline read, "IBC NEWS ANCHOR SUSAN MCCALUM & UNIDENTIFIED PASSENGER KILLED IN ONE CAR ROLL-OVER ACCIDENT ON I-45."

After reading this he yelled, "Jo! Come quick! You won't believe this!"

She came running out of the bathroom while pulling a comb through her wet hair and exclaimed, "What? What's wrong?"

"McCalum from IBC and an unidentified passenger were killed in a wreck on Interstate 45!"

Jo dropped the comb as her arms fell limp to her sides. "Oh my God," she muttered.

Rick asked, "Do you think Jason was with her?"

In a soft voice Jo said, "I hope not. Let's get over to Ted's office and find out if he knows anything more."

The drive to Ted's office was somber and deliberate. Still wearing her sling, Jo drove, since she figured whatever Rick had mixed into his coffee could be a problem if he got behind the wheel.

Rick tuned on a radio news station along the way, and they heard a report that the passenger killed with Susan McCalum had been identified as one of the IBC producers.

Jo and Rick looked at each other with an uneasy feeling of relief, but neither one said a word as they pulled through the security gates at Ted's office. Two lives had been lost under suspicious circumstances, and Jason was still unaccounted for.

As the two scientists approached Ted's office, they could hear a muffled, repeating thump coming from behind the closed door.

Jo knocked, and they heard Ted call out, "Come in!"

Opening the door, they saw Ted behind his desk, facing the wall. He appeared to be playing a game of catch by tossing a tennis ball against the wall behind his desk.

Jo closed the door behind them, and they each quietly took a seat. Ted stopped thumping the ball against the wall and turned to face them.

"Have you heard?" he asked.

Jo opened her cell phone and pulled up the text message Jason sent to her. She then handed it over the desk to Ted as she said, "Jason sent this to me last night, but I didn't see it until this morning."

Looking at the message Ted said, "Security watched him send this message from the lab, just before he sent his video clip of Hydravitric to Susan McCalum at IBC."

Handing the phone back to Jo, Ted asked, "Do you know how he ended his demonstration?"

"No, he didn't copy me on what he sent," Jo responded.

"To the best of our knowledge, what I'm about to show you two never got to Susan McCalum at IBC. She received a call from Jason, and was expecting something to be sent, but security blocked his smartphone message before it ever got to her."

Rick looked at Jo, then back at Ted and asked, "So was her car wreck really an accident?"

Ted tossed the tennis ball across the room and made a bank-shot into the wastebasket near the door.

"Believe it or not, her accident appears to be just that. She may have been on her way to try and find out why she never got Jason's message, but to our knowledge, there was no outside influence with what happened."

This didn't reassure Jo or Rick, since Ted's use of the phrase 'to our knowledge' reminded them both of their earlier discussion about 'plausible ignorance.' They remembered that when an authority figure is purposefully kept out of the loop, they could truthfully say they had no knowledge of the matter.

Ted then turned the flat screen on his desktop computer toward Jo and Rick, and brought up a paused video clip.

Jason was seated in the lab, pointing toward a large glass bowl filled with water. He had pointed his smartphone camera at himself, so the viewer could see what he was about to do.

Riveted by the sight of their long-time friend and colleague, Jo and Rick both slid to the edge of their seats and leaned forward to get a closer look.

"I need to warn you both that what you're about to see is seriously disturbing. Jason shows us what Hydravitric does to liquid water, then he does something you'd never expect."

Hitting the enter key to start the video, Ted slid his chair back from his desk and looked away.

Jason leaned toward the camera and said, "This is being sent to demonstrate a new force of nature we discovered with the Starsweep space mission. Material brought back to Earth from the Johnson-Taylor Comet turns liquid water into sand, and this fact is being hidden from the public! Can't believe it? Watch this."

Jason opened a short, glass vial that appears to contain small, ash-like grains of Hydravitric. Shaking it over the bowl of water, the liquid can be clearly seen transforming into sand in a matter of seconds.

Looking into the camera again, Jason stated, "Scary as this is, it's a reality in nature, and I think everyone has the need, and the right, to know about it.

We call it Hydravitric, and the people trying to hide this are the same ones trying to keep the European satellite from bringing more of it back to Earth. They think keeping this a secret is the right thing to do, but it explains so many mysteries about where water went on Mars, and why there is so little liquid water found other places in our solar system. It's too important to hide!

I wish I had time to say more, but they don't want this to get out, and they're after me. I can only think of one way out that would be tough for them to explain this away as a trick video, just created for publicity.

This stuff is out there, and the world needs to know about it! Mom, Dad, family and friends, I love you all, and may God have mercy on our souls."

With that, Jason tilted back his head, raised the vial above his open mouth, and shook the remaining contents out.

In an instant, Jason's body began to transform into what looked like a sandstone replica of his image. A faint, anguished cry could be heard fading as the figure began to crumble under its own weight, into a pile of ashen sand.

Tears streamed down both Jo and Rick's cheeks as they turned away from the horrible spectacle, and Rick uttered, "Heaven help us."

Ted looked back at Jo and Rick to say, "Only a small handful of people have seen this video, and those on the Security Council that have, insist that all traces of the message be destroyed. The President has yet to make that decision, and we may never know if that happens.

We don't believe anyone at IBC saw it, so the secret remains safe."

With a look of doubt on his face, Rick asked Ted, "How did he send a video out if he's gone?"

"It appears he created a phone App that sent out the video by linking the file with a delay timer, and a call list."

Wiping away her tears, Jo asked, "Did Jason destroy all of the material?"

"Unfortunately, we're not sure of that. During the early testing, we seem to have lost track of the amounts used versus what was brought back in the Starsweep. No more can be found in the lab, but that doesn't mean Jason might not have done something else with any that might remain."

"And what's the status of the European satellite right now?" Rick asked.

"Tonight at about nine o'clock our time, their craft will enter Earth's atmosphere over the south Atlantic. If it lands in water, it's anybody's guess what will happen. If it comes down over the ice pack of the Antarctic, there's a chance we'll be spared a gruesome end.

European space officials are in constant contact with us at this point. They also believe it's imperative that what we know about Hydravitric remains a secret.

I know how hard you have worked on this project, and with everything that's been happening, I'm not sure there's any good way to tell you this, so I'm just going to lay it out.

The Starsweep research program is being officially shut down, and a media release will say funding has been cut, because we feel we've learned all we can from the material brought back from the mission.

You will both be assigned new project responsibilities at NASA, and the bottom line is that none of this ever happened. If we survive tonight's landing in the south Atlantic, Hydravitric never existed.

If any part of what's occurred with all this gets out to the public, it will be played down by the government and the 'powers-that-be' in the media, as a baseless hoax.

I suggest we all go home and try to get some rest, and if you're so inclined, say a prayer that tomorrow's sunrise brings just another day."

Jo slammed her fist on Ted's desk, and with a stern stare leaned forward. Through gritted teeth she said, "That's it? We're shutting it down? A new force of nature is discovered, and we're going to pretend it doesn't exist?"

Looking down, Ted shook his head from side to side and said, "I wish things were different Jo, but all we can do is follow orders and deal with it. If we dodge this bullet tonight, and Hydravitric doesn't put an ugly end to life as we know it, those making these critical decisions believe the world will be better off not knowing about it."

Rick gruffly interjected, "So they've decided that what the people don't know can't hurt them."

"In a nutshell, that's what it boils down to. And who are we to disagree?" Ted asked.

Looking at his watch, he said, "I promised my wife and kids we'd do lunch and go to the zoo this afternoon, so we need to end this.

A handful of people on this planet know that whatever happens tonight could forever change the course of history.

Go be with your family and friends.

God willing, I'll be in touch."

Jo and Rick slowly stood, turned, and left Ted's office without saying another word.

As they walked to Jo's car, she asked Rick, "Do you think Jason really used it all up?"

"If we're lucky he did, but if you recall his story about Hercules, wasn't the immortal head of the Hydra hidden under a rock for later use against another foe?

Considering what we know about decisions made by those in charge, I wouldn't put it past them to still have some of the comet dust hidden away somewhere."

"If they bring more Hydravitric safely back to Earth tonight with the European craft, what do you think they will do with it?" Rick wondered with a tremble in his voice.

As they got into the car, Jo replied, "You mean if we're lucky, and it doesn't turn the oceans into desert? I'm not sure. Using it all up at once in a container of some sort might be the safest option. My biggest fear is that someone will want to keep it around for use as a weapon. I remember Jason listing some possible 'good' uses it might have, but we all know the risks of destroying Earth's precious water resources far out-weigh any useful reasons to keep it around."

As Jo drove out of the parking lot to take Rick back to his place, she told him her plans to talk to her folks before the landing occurred.

She knew she couldn't tell them what could happen if the E.U. craft landed in the ocean, but she felt they should know the project was being canceled, and she wanted to let them know how much their love and support has meant to her.

Rick shared that he planned to call his family members, too. They both knew it would be the most difficult calls they would probably ever make, since they had no way of knowing what the landing outcome would be, and they could not tell anyone about the potential peril.

That night, the European craft came down over the remote south Atlantic, with very little attention paid by the media. As it re-entered Earth's atmosphere, radar and satellite tracking instruments indicated that it split apart into three sections.

One piece was lost over the water, and sank to the frigid ocean depths, never to be recovered. That particular section wasn't thought to contain any of the comet material, but the only evidence was that no transformation of water to sand took place.

The other two parts came down over the Antarctic, and scattered over several hundred square miles of mountainous snowpack, and ice.

There were no catastrophic news reports of water changing to sand, but the people who knew how the material acts also knew that it has no effect on frozen water.

Given what could have happened if the craft had landed in water, Jo felt God chose to give the Earth another chance. Perhaps with Jason's help, Hercules had once again defeated the Hydra.

EPILOGUE

Over time, Jo and Rick had been reassigned and gone about their new research duties. They also swore to keep what they knew about the Starsweep project secret.

Military and research personnel who were present during the remote lake test knew nothing about the nature of what was being investigated. They only knew it was classified Top Secret, and as such, could not be revealed to anyone for fear of prosecution, imprisonment, or being declared insane and sent to a mental hospital.

To this day, teams of scientists and researchers who live and work on the Antarctic continent are still searching for debris from the European spacecraft, and they gather rock specimens found on and under, the snow and ice surface.

These specimens are simply identified as meteorites from space. Few people know where these samples are taken once they are collected, or what happens to them after they are collected.

When Jo or Rick would hear or read, strange news stories about whole whale skeletons being found in the shifting sands of a desert, they knew a simple explanation existed. They also knew the truth was being hidden.

Photos returned from numerous past Mars missions have shown that large amounts of water once existed on the Martian surface. Unfortunately, the pictures offered no evidence of why the rivers, lakes, and seas have all disappeared. The only evidence of moisture there now is the presence of drifting snow and frozen icecaps. With what they know about Hydravitric, this all makes sense, but they cannot share it with anyone.

Jo sometimes wonders if legend and folklore surrounding the lost continent of Atlantis might be explained if a sea surrounding it suddenly became desert. Over the centuries, would its' existence be lost under the ever-shifting sands? Some have searched for remnants of Atlantis under the oceans, but given what the NASA scientists know now, they may have been looking in all the wrong places. Perhaps long ago it was entombed under what is now land.

Without warning, could the Earth still be transformed into a dry desert?

Only those with full knowledge of the Starsweep project have had to live with this nightmare in the back of their minds.

Scientists have long known that a number of natural disasters could one-day cause unimaginable devastation. These include the fear that near-Earth asteroids will impact our planet.

Other looming disasters include a long-overdue, massive earthquake along the U.S. west coast's San Andreas Fault, or an eruption of the world's largest volcanic caldera, which is known as Yellowstone.

As devastating as any of these events would be, they pale in comparison to what hell would be caused by the unleashing of Hydravitric.

No natural or man-made disaster, as we understand them today, would even come close to what it would mean to lose the world's water supply.

The remote polar rock collection activities continue to this day, and there is growing concern about the longer seasonal thaw cycles that have been observed. This is because they could bring undiscovered Hydravitric into contact with runoff streams that flow toward the open ocean.

Sophisticated new sensing instruments have been developed to locate very small fragments of rocky material found on or below the snow and ice-covered terrain. Scientists using them have not been told the truth about why these devices are needed.

People doing surface collection and transport of specimens are carefully trained in the handling of the material, but they have no idea what these specimens are suspected to be, where they are taken, or what is being done with them. They are taught that it is critical that the material never gets wet, but they are told this is to avoid contamination of experiments. They have no idea what the real consequences would be.

Only those in charge of the never-ending search know that even a trace of this material getting into a major waterway could mean the end.

As time has passed, Jo and Rick have learned to live with the situation, much the same way we all go about our daily lives without worrying about other dangers in nature that we have no control over.

One afternoon, about two years after the European craft landing was little more than a footnote in history, Jo received a call from Rick.

"Did you see the news item that was briefly on the IBC website, about a tomb discovered in Egypt? A unique urn with odd markings was found. The vessel was dropped, and when it broke open, a small stone fell out.

When a sweating archeologist picked it up, take a guess what the report said happened to him..."

Jo dropped the phone.

"Jo, are you there? Hello? Are you okay? Jo!"

About The Authors

Over a ten-year span, "Hidden Thirst" became a creative writing venture by the father-daughter team of Doug and Amy Palmer. They decided to work together on writing an adventure story based on science realities and fiction fantasies.

The story evolved as they discussed current events in science and space exploration, while continually asking each other, "What if?"

Doug is a Product Designer and Educator, with a Master of Arts in Communication. Amy holds a business degree in Marketing and International Business, as well as a minor in Spanish Studies.

They are proud to be Cheeseheads from Wisconsin, and hope the audience finds their story is as much fun to read, as it was to write!

2002   2012